Body in the Woods

Body in the Woods

Sarah Lotz

NewCon Press
England

First published in the UK by NewCon Press
41 Wheatsheaf Road, Alconbury Weston, Cambs, PE28 4LF
August 2017

NCP 127 (limited edition hardback)
NCP 128 (softback)

10 9 8 7 6 5 4 3 2 1

ISBN:

978-1-910935-51-4 (hardback)
978-1-910935-52-1 (softback)

Cover art by Vincent Sammy
Cover layout by Andy Bigwood

Minor editorial meddling by Ian Whates
Book layout by Storm Constantine

One

It's getting on for eleven when something triggers the motion detector light outside the front door. The light pooling into the lounge dies after five seconds but, next to me, Manchee's gone rigid. She whines, slinks off the couch and heads for the door. I mute the blather on the telly – I've been half-watching an Adam Sandler movie on Netflix, the kind of shite I indulge in when Iain's away – and listen hard, trying to dampen the flicker of irrational fear. You'd have to be a particularly tenacious home invader to schlep all the way out here to break in, but tonight I'm twitchier than usual. For the last three days the rain hasn't let up, a sullen downpour that's set me on edge and made working in the garden a misery.

The light clicks on again. *Just a fox. It's just a fox.* The garden is teeming with wildlife large enough to trigger the sensor, and I should be used to it by now.

Five, four, three, two, one. Darkness.

I breathe out.

Then, audible over the spatter-shush of the rain, comes: *Crunch. Crunch, crunch.* It can only be one thing – footsteps on the gravel path.

Crunch.

I scoot to the window and peer into the garden beyond. Something shifts in the darkness next to the pyramid shadows of the new evergreen shrubs. The light flares again. A bulky figure is standing there, its back to me. Whoever it is – and it's a man, definitely a man – is wearing a hooded rain slicker like a character out of a slasher movie. Wait… there's a familiar slant to the shoulders. He's too tall for Colin, the farmer who lives at the top of the lane, too bulky for George, my friend Samantha's husband. He crunches away, disappearing around the corner where my jeep is parked, then returns.

Manchee barks again and scratches at the door. She's a medium-sized dog, a rescue; I've only had her for four months, and I have no idea if she'll protect me if it comes down to it.

Why doesn't he knock on the door?

Because he's casing the joint, The Fear whispers.

I run through my options: call the police; call Sam and George; Skype Iain in Doha.

Stop being such a wimp, and woman-up. You know this person. They might need help.

I look around for a weapon, then tell myself to stop being paranoid. I open up before The Fear wins, Manchee springing past me into the night. The rain slants silver in the light above the porch, momentarily blinding me. 'Hello?'

Nothing. *Crunch*, then: 'Claire?'

The figure slides off its hood.

'*Dean?*'

'Yeah.' He darts forward to give me a peck on the cheek. 'Can I come in?'

I find my voice. 'Of course.' I stand back to let him squeeze past me. He's soaking, and he tracks mud across the wooden floor. I haven't seen Dean since we shared a sneaky drink in London just before Iain and I bought this place – almost a year ago now. Blood heats my face at the memory, and I'm aware I'm in my PJs and slippers, I haven't showered for two days, and I look, quite simply, like crap. The cottage still reeks of the ox heart I cooked for Manchee's supper, a sour, meaty odour that clings to the walls. Iain can't stand it: 'Why don't you just open a can for her?' he always asks. But I like doing it. Manchee sits and waits patiently while I slice through the coating of stubborn yellow fat and fry it, her eyes never leaving the plate when I set it to cool. *Why are you thinking about this now, Claire?*

Speak. 'What are you doing here, Dean?' He can't be "just dropping by". The cottage is set in a warren of unmarked country roads and the top of the driveway is little more than a gap in the hedgerow. I have to give visitors – even local delivery people – painfully detailed directions and Dean has never been here.

'Have you got something to drink?' he asks. Despite living in London for years, he's still kept his Glasgow accent. And his appearance hasn't changed: his longish black hair, blue eyes, and laughter lines have stayed the same since I first met him. People always stare at Dean; he's not fabulously good-looking – he's a character actor rather than a leading man – but there's something about him.

'Of course. Um… Iain's away, working in Qatar.'

'I know.'

'How?'

'You put it on your Facebook.' I forgot he was on it – he never posts anything. Is this why he's here? Because Iain's away? I'm not sure how to feel about this. 'Nice place you've got here,' he says. 'You've done well for yourself, so you have.' But he's not really looking at the room. His eyes are glassy – is he drunk?

'Thanks. We're still doing it up. Spent the last six months on the cottage, next are the outbuildings. We're converting them. I'm thinking of putting them on AirBnB. Holiday lets.' *Babble, babble, toil and trouble.*

'Mae always said you were going to do that someday.'

'Did she?'

'Sure she did. Don't you remember? She said you'd be suited to fixing up an old place, a scarf tied around your hair.' Finally he

7

smiles. *No. He's not drunk. It's something else.*

'How did you even find this place?' I ask. *And why didn't you call to let me know you were coming? Why didn't you email me?*

'You sent me the link to the property listing the last time we met, remember? The Rightmove link.'

'Of course I did.' A twinge of guilt. I hadn't told Iain I was meeting Dean that day. Dean had emailed me, asked if I wanted to meet him for a catch-up session, and I'd said yes. A slide down to London, a couple of pints, the hectic *Italian Job* run for the train home – there are only a couple that go to Morton-on-Spay. Three-and-a-half hours each way, and all for an hour of stolen time. I've forgotten what lie I'd told Iain.

He gives me another unconvincing grin. 'So how about that drink, then?'

Dean follows me into the kitchen, where I dig through the cupboards looking for booze. These days I only allow myself to drink when I go out and we're not set up for unexpected guests. A tray of congealed fat, the remains of last night's sausages, sits accusingly on the stove. Manchee sniffs Dean's shoes, and he makes a fuss of her, calling her a 'good girl' and asking her name. I unearth some sloe gin Iain's brother gave us last Christmas, the bottle dusty and sticky. I fumble to open it. Dean takes it from me and untwists the cap. For the first time I notice he's wearing gloves – expensive-looking, soft leather gloves.

'So Iain's away,' he says. It's not a question.

'Yes. Two more weeks.'

'Enjoying the work, is he?'

'Not really, but it pays well.' God, this is awkward. I've never had such a stilted conversation with Dean before. There's something hanging in the air between us.

'How's Jake doing?' he asks.

'Fine. He's enjoying Edinburgh, and the course is going well.' My mouth is dry. Truth is, I haven't spoken to my son for more than a month.

I pour us both a glass and make myself go through the small

talk motions. 'And how's Zack?' It's a thorny subject. The last I'd heard, Dean's son had dropped out of university. Dean doesn't answer. 'Dean... has something happened?'

'Yes.'

And something's happening to his bottom lip. It's trembling. He wipes the heel of his hand over it. It steadies.

Dread smarms into my gut. 'Is Zack okay, Dean? Is it Mae?'

'I need your help, Claire.'

'Are you in trouble?' There's a heavy silence. My heart is thudding. This is all wrong. 'Dean?'

'It's best if I show you. You'll need a coat.'

'Show me?'

'It's outside.'

'What's outside?'

'Trust me, Claire, you need to see this for yourself.'

He downs the drink and stands by the back door. I scrabble in the boot room, grabbing a waterproof at random – one of Iain's. It smells of the cigarettes he sneaks occasionally. I thrust my hands in the pockets and touch the gossamer remains of a tissue, the cracked rectangle of an old lighter.

There are a thousand questions I should ask, but I don't.

I follow Dean outside, and around the side of the house. The sensor light clicks on, but this time I'm glad of it. He's parked his car next to my old faithful Suzuki jeep. It's a huge white sedan, a Mercedes, the paintwork jewelled with rain. Dean always had the best cars, the best houses, the best stuff. *Style but no substance*, Iain calls it. I'm surprised I didn't hear him approaching. Our driveway is long, but I usually hear engine noise; this place collects sounds greedily, as if it's aware it hasn't got much to work with. A bat zigs above our heads.

'So? What is it, Dean?'

He opens the boot and stands back.

I peer down at a long form that at first glance resembles a rolled carpet. It's wrapped in thick plastic and bent in the middle to fit in the space. The brown masking tape sealing the plastic

clinches it in here and there to form an unmistakable shape.
It's not a carpet.
It's a body.

TWO

Back, back in time I go, sifting through memories, dredging up the first time I encountered Dean. Back, back to that Friday evening, eight – almost nine – years ago, when Jake ran into the flat after school, and before he even said hello, blurted: 'Zack wants me to sleepover tonight.'

'Who's Zack?'

'The new kid. My mate.'

I didn't say, *You have a friend? Oh thank* fuck. Instead, I gaped at him.

'Can I go?'

'You *want* to go?'

'Duh, Mom, course.'

'Where does he live?'

'Here.' Jake gave me a scrap of paper with a phone number written on it. He dumped his schoolbag on the counter, said, 'Can I go play Tomb Raider?' and scooted off without waiting for an answer. I dialled, ripping a piece of flesh off my thumb with my teeth as I did so – social anxiety rearing its ugly head as usual. *Don't screw this up, Claire. A friend, he's made a friend.* Could this be an end to the tears before school, the dirty suspicion that he was being bullied?

The phone was answered on the first ring: 'This is Mae.' In the background I could hear some kind of music – jazz, probably.

'Um. Hi, Mae. This is Claire. Jake's mother.' My thumb was bleeding. I sucked it.

A pause, then: 'Oh *hey*, Claire. So the boys want to hang out tonight. That okay with you? I tell you, Zack never stops talking about Jake.'

'Are you sure?'

'Of course I'm sure. Hey, why don't you come over, have a drink, check the place out. Make sure we're not perverts.' She laughed. Her voice was masculine, sexy, smoky, American. I said yes. Of course I did.

They lived in a Victorian semi at the end of my favourite street, one of those characterful properties with leaded windows and an elegant porch that smelled of old wood. Mae greeted Jake and me like old friends and waved us inside. I'd seen her once outside the school gates on one of the days I didn't have to work. She was older than most of the other parents, and looked vaguely North African. She was tall and skinny – almost to the point of emaciation. Her wrists were tiny. I felt like an elephant next to her.

'Zack's in his room, hon,' she said to Jake. 'Go on up, second door to the left.'

'Cool.' He disappeared without glancing at me for reassurance.

'Come and have a drink.' She wafted me into the kitchen, and en route I caught a glimpse of rooms filled with books and light and exotic throw rugs. It was a cruel contrast to my flat, with its chipboard, fitted carpets and lack of anything approaching character. The image of that house lodged in my mind of course. I wanted it with a longing that bordered on the pathological. I wanted warm wood, colourful rugs. I wanted books and a wood-burning stove. It was a home, not just a place in which to sleep and eat and shit.

By now I was sweating. The mascara I'd hastily applied felt as if it was forming dark circles under my eyes. My cheap top made my skin itch. 'Your house is lovely, Mae.'

'You think? Not sure about it yet.'

A bottle of white wine sat on the counter, the glass beaded with condensation. She poured me a glass. 'Cheers.' She smiled at me, showing off small skewed teeth. She was elegant, cosmopolitan, out of place in this workaday town.

'What the hell are you doing here?' I blurted. 'Sorry – that came out wrong. I mean in this area.'

Mae laughed. 'I'm lecturing at the university.' She wrinkled her nose. 'Gender and violence.'

'Wow.' I gulped the wine, coughed. 'And you're from the States?'

'The U.S? Originally yeah. Been living in London for the last ten years, then here.'

'How long have you been here?'

'Couple of months. Still settling in. But enough about me, tell me all about you.'

Mae didn't do small talk. We got straight into it, trading back-stories in the first ten minutes. I had Jake when I was eighteen. Mae fell unexpectedly pregnant when she was forty. We were stranded either side of the mummy divide. She was too old to fit in; I was too young. And we had other things in common: both of us had moved into the area fairly recently; both of us were struggling with the move, albeit for different reasons. I lied and told her I was an artist rather than what I actually was – a glorified house painter – and tried to make Jamie, the man I'd been living with for the last couple of years, sound interesting. She was blunt and funny and cool and out of my league and I desperately wanted her to like me. I began to relax; or maybe the wine was going to my head.

A thunder of feet and Jake and Zack rushed in. Zack was as

slender as his mother. He shook my hand like a grown-up. I liked him immediately.

'Can we get ice-cream, Mom?' His accent was pure South London.

'Sure, hon. Help yourself.'

He nudged Jake and they both laughed. Jake zooted up to me, flung his arms around me and kissed me the cheek. 'I love it here,' he said. 'I love you.'

I almost dropped my glass. Mae picked up on my shock and winked at me. It had been months since I'd seen Jake looking so happy. The kids ran off.

'Where's his father?' Mae asked.

I wasn't ready to get into that right then, so I mumbled something about him being out of the picture.

She gave me a shrewd glance. 'Come and meet Dean.'

She led me through glass doors and out in the garden. It was early summer, and the lawn and artfully overgrown flowerbeds were dappled in a hazy glow. I breathed in the scent of honeysuckle. There was no traffic noise.

Dean was sitting at a wooden table, tapping at a laptop.

'Dean,' Mae said. 'This is Jake's mom.'

Dean looked up. I took in crinkly eyes, a shock of black hair and stylish reading glasses balanced on his nose. He gave me a slow smile, as if he was really seeing me, and something shifted inside me. 'I'm so glad we found you,' he said. And that was it. From that moment on, I was theirs; they were mine.

There was something off about Mae and Dean's relationship, but it would be years before I'd find out what it was.

Three

I don't scream. Is it the shock?

There's a bulbous eiderdown or duvet beneath the plastic smothering the body, which to some extent obscures its exact shape. It could be a man or a woman.

Mae, is this Mae?

No. There's a shoe in the corner of the car's trunk: a trainer – a man's. Adidas. Does – *did* – the shoe belong to the body? It's not Dean's. He wouldn't be seen dead in trainers. The Dean I knew had an immaculate, Parisian sense of style: Cleverly draped scarves in winter, leather shoes. I have never seen him in shorts or jeans. And even now, it hits me that his raincoat is elegantly cut. He dresses like someone who has money, but he, like me, comes from nothing. I'm one of the few people who know this.

Still I ask, half-hopeful: 'Is this some kind of prank, Dean?'

'No.'

Of course it's not a fucking prank. 'Who is it, Dean?'

'Let's go back inside.'

A rush of white noise, a gush in my ears, and then: *Run.* Run. But before I can act on this, Dean grips my elbow, and steers me back into the cottage. I barely feel the gravel beneath my slippers.

But more than this, it's the past between us that anchors me.

It's not cold, but I shiver. I force my hands back into my pockets; grip the tissue. I'm lightheaded. There's a scratching sound coming from somewhere. I block it out.

'Who is he, Dean?' He doesn't answer me. 'Who is the man in the trunk?' The thoughts are coming thick and fast. Perhaps he was drink-driving, knocked someone over. An accident, and he needs to cover it up. I shake the thought away – it's too close to home. '*Dean.*'

A long pause, and then he stares into my eyes. 'The less you know the better, Claire.'

Ask it, ask it, ask it. I swallow, and taste salt and old pennies. 'Did you kill him?'

'No! Of course not. How could you ask that?'

'How can I *ask* that? There's a body in your fucking car!'

A brief purse of the lips at my swear word. Dean never swears, which has always struck me as odd – and particularly odd right now. 'I didn't kill him. That's all you need to know.'

What if… what if he turns on you next? What if Dean is some kind of deranged killer?

No. You know him. Dean would never …

I fight to sound rational: 'Look, Dean. I… Look, I don't know what's happened here, but you have to go to the police.'

He pours us another drink, taking over the kitchen with his usual easy grace and confidence. The twitchiness from earlier has gone. 'I can't, Claire. You have to trust me on this.'

'*Trust* you?'

'Is that so hard?'

'What's his name?'

'Eh?'

'The body. What's the man's name?'

He shuts his eyes. 'He's no one.'

'Everyone's someone, Dean.' *Somebody's husband. Somebody's son.* I shudder. That's the title of a book about a serial killer isn't it?

I down the sloe gin. It sits there in my throat like muck in a drain.

'You have to trust me here, Claire. The less you know the better.'

That sound again. Then I get what it is: Manchee's scratching at the door. I've shut her outside in the rain. I let her in, stumbling as I do so. My legs are heavy; my body is absorbing the shock of the situation even if my brain hasn't quite caught up.

'You should sit, Claire. You're looking pale.'

'No shit.'

He gently pushes me into a chair. A chair I bought for next to nothing from an auction, and lovingly sandpapered down and painted. I'd been so proud of it, but really, it's just tat. For an instant, the old cottage, with its lime-washed stonewalls, grumbling Rayburn, and the wooden floors Iain and I sanded and sealed, seems tawdry. The wood too yellow; the walls too bright. A poor facsimile of the home in which I'd first met Mae and the man now standing in my kitchen.

He pours me a third drink and puts it in my hand.

'What... Why did you bring him here, Dean?' *You know why.*

'We can bury him in the woods. There's miles of them around here, aren't there?' He makes this sound almost reasonable.

'How did he die, Dean? I have to know.'

'No questions, Claire. If we're going to do this thing, we need to do it now. We're running out of time here.' I check the clock. Almost midnight. *When corpses in the trunk turn into pumpkins.* Time is operating on a different plane. He lowers his voice. 'And do you not remember what you said to me once?'

I stare at him blankly.

'That night you came round after that idiot of a boyfriend left you. James. No, Jamie. We were talking about friendship. What makes someone a good friend.'

'I have no idea what ...'

Then it comes back. Woolly at first, then in more clarity. Me all cried out, sitting at his kitchen table, drunk on brandy, and someone – me? *Was* it me? – saying something like: *The definition of a good friend is agreeing to help them dispose of a body, no questions asked.*

'I wasn't serious, Dean.'

'Is that so? Well, I'm calling your bluff, Claire. You going to help me or not?'

He doesn't say: you owe me, Claire. He doesn't need to. We both know it.

Four

No one tells you how much it hurts. I've read about people dying from a broken heart, but I didn't expect it to happen to me.

I lay on the couch, numb with pain and disbelief. It had come out of the blue that morning. Jamie, the man I'd thought was my soul mate, had sat up in bed and said: 'I'm not happy.'

I went instantly cold – I remember that. 'What?'

'I'm not happy.'

'What? Why?'

'It's not working out.'

We'd been together for two years. Jake had even started calling him 'dad' for fuck sakes. And then it all poured out. He wasn't ready for this. For being part of a ready-made family. Deep down I must have known it was coming. He'd been withdrawing from us for months – barely listening when I vented my worries about Jake, and making excuses to go out with his friends almost every night.

I watched, sickened, while he packed up his stuff. He glanced at me on the way out. 'You'll be fine, Claire. You've got your mates.'

'My *mates?*' He knew full well that I'd given up the city I loved, my friends, and my family to move to his hometown and be with him. But he'd timed it right, I had to give him that. Jake was away for a couple of days on a school trip. Jamie could slip away with the minimum amount of fuss.

I had a job that day: a kitchen revamp. I was scratching a living refurbishing furniture and interiors, and I called in sick. I half-watched daytime TV, a vomit of Jeremy Kyle and *Trisha* and property makeover programmes, while I drowned in self-pity. *Why do they always leave?* Jake's dad didn't count. We were never together.

Along with the pain came the worry: now what? Financially, I couldn't make ends meet on my own. The rent would swallow more than half of what I usually made. Jamie didn't bring in much, but enough to help. I couldn't ask my parents again; they'd made it clear that they were tapped out. I'd have to go back on the dole. I could move back to Birmingham, but that would mean ripping Jake out of school, taking him away from his one and only friend. The only people I had were Mae and Dean. On the day that Jamie dropped his bomb, I'd known them for three months.

It was Mae's comfort I was looking for as I zombie-shuffled to their house, tear-stained, unwashed and shaking, but it was Dean who answered the door. Mae wasn't in. I'd forgotten she was away at an academic conference. I'd never been alone with Dean before. Up till then, he was little more than an intriguing background fixture, an oddly sexy man who suavely popped in and out on mysterious errands. I found him both charming and intimidating; he was so self-assured. Mae had told me he was an accountant (adding, cryptically, 'but he's very creative') who specialised in the entertainment industry – his clients were actors, production companies, directors. It sounded impossibly glamorous. Mae had dropped hints that all was not well in her marriage, but I hadn't yet seen any sign of it.

Dean didn't act surprised when I washed up on his doorstep. He silently wheeled me in, sat me at the kitchen table, and handed me a glass of brandy. I was past feeling embarrassed at a relative stranger seeing me in such a state. I wanted to cry, and he let me.

The first thing he said to me that day was: 'It won't feel like this forever, Claire.'

I spoke to him for hours. He listened. Allowing someone to see your emotional underbelly seals a friendship. Dean saw me at my most vulnerable, and he didn't flinch. It created a bond, a dangerous one, I suppose, although I didn't know that then.

I talked and drank, and drank and talked. He didn't try anything on with me, although I wouldn't have stopped him if he had. We stayed up until it got light. I know we spoke about friendship and loyalty. But here's the thing: I don't remember saying 'The definition of a good friend is agreeing to help them dispose of a body, no questions asked'. It's not the kind of thing I would say, even when drunk. I think it was Dean who said that. I'm almost sure of it.

You can still change your mind.

But I don't. I dig out Iain's old boots and waterproofs to give to Dean, and pull on my wellies – the stupid cartoon ones I bought from Aldi. I mentally scrawl a list of what we'll need: a pick. A shovel. Gloves. Flashlights… A shopping list for digging a grave.

At the back of my mind there's a voice bleating, *don't do this, Claire. Don't. You can't take it back. Don't don't don't.* So why do I carry on? Why, when I say to Dean, 'Move the body to the back of my car, we'll have to take the logging roads and I can't risk us getting stuck', does my voice sound strong and sure, as if burying a corpse is what I do every day, along with digging the compost pit and feeding the dog?

I hurry back to the cottage to fetch the flashlights and gloves while Dean wrangles with the body. *What if it's got rigor mortis and is locked into position?* Jesus. I can't watch him doing it. I can't.

Back in the kitchen I lean over the sink. I gag, but nothing comes up. I look at my reflection in the darkened window. Shadows accentuate my jowls; my face looks as if it's melting.

Don't do this, Claire.

I've been walking in the forest that surrounds my house almost every day since we bought the place. That's eleven months now. How many walks? A hundred? Two hundred? I've got to know the place; the snaking tracks, the shortcuts, the deer paths, the dips and the eyries, the areas where the shafts of light shine down through the pine trees. I've seen deer, owls, foxes and rabbits, each time with the child-like fascination of someone who grew up in an inner city flat. I have been stung, I've got lost, and I've fallen over many times. It's my corner of the Earth. The clouds of midges, the mud, the soft comforting hum of loam and pine, the sound of my breathing, the crack of a boot on frozen grass: it's all mine. I've surprised myself by how much I love the woods – I've never thought of myself as an outdoors person.

If I do this thing, they'll be ruined for me. Stained.

Don't do this, Claire. Call the police. Call George, he'll know what to do.

And how *does* someone end up with a body in the trunk of their car? *Could* it be a drink-driving incident he needs to cover up? No. He's sober, and for some reason I have the impression that the body is a recent development, not something that he's been hiding for a while. Could he have attacked someone in a rage? No. I can't see that. I've never seen him lose his temper or raise his voice, not even with Mae. Perhaps he's involved with a married woman, and they planned the murder of her husband together. No. Dean wouldn't be that stupid, and this isn't a fucking Nicolas Cage B movie.

Don't do it.

But he provided a lifeline when I needed one most. And Zack... Zack had done the same for my little boy when he was drowning. I can't deny this.

If you do this, you can't take it back.

I know.

I pull on a pair of gardening gloves and go back outside to collect the tools from the workroom, the rain spitting on my hood. I can't find the fork, then remember leaving it next to the nettle patch. I stumble around for several minutes in the dark until I find it. When I make it back to the car, Dean is breathing hard. The corpse is now in the back of my jeep. What I assume to be the feet are propped up against the side window to make it fit. Iain removed the back seats to provide more space for Manchee, but what would he say if he could see the grim cargo the car was now carrying?

What would he say if he knew Dean were here?

I estimate that the man must have been fairly short – five eight or nine probably, although it's hard to tell exactly under the layers, and I can't bring myself to look too closely. And here's another question: where the hell did Dean get that plastic sheeting? Who has that kind of thing hanging around?

Builders and serial killers.

Manchee dances next to the car. She's ecstatic: *We're going for a walk? What, now?*

Should I lock her in the house? No. If someone spots the car I can use her as an excuse, 'Couldn't sleep, thought I'd take Manchee out for a walk'. Or maybe I'll say she ran off, and I'm trying to find her. Yes, that's reasonable. She's always haring off after squirrels and rabbits.

We can bury the body in the woods. But where? Where? Where?

The second I stow the tools in the back, Manchee jumps in. She sniffs the body, then sits calmly next to it, head cocked, tongue lolling, waiting. I breathe in deeply. I can't detect a whiff of decomposition. The only scents are wet dog and the mouldy reek that has inhabited the old car since I bought it.

I climb into the driver's seat. Wait. I'm forgetting something. *Your sanity?* The torches. I left them next to the sink. Without saying anything to Dean, I run back to the cottage.

When I leave, I lock the front door behind me, something I don't usually bother to do.

I back up the driveway, Dean sitting silently beside me, the car's de-mister whirring overtime to clear the condensation on the inside of the windscreen. The wipers are old and clack against the glass, a dull metronome.

'How old is he, Dean?' I haven't planned to ask this, it just comes out.

'Huh?'

'The man. The body. How old?'

Dean places a hand on my thigh. I slap it away. I don't want him to touch me. 'Claire,' he says, dodging the question. 'I know this is a big ask.'

'Yeah.'

The engine sounds like a howl in the quiet of night. *Don't panic, no one will hear us.* There are the livery stables a mile up the road, but they're hidden from view, and the two posh and terrifying women who run them should be fast asleep by now. Then there's Colin's farm at the top, but the driveway leading to his place is long and winding, so it's unlikely he'll hear us either. Then there's nothing but miles and miles of logging tracks, walking paths and the mountain bike trails. *The ideal place to stash a body.* The jeep skids as I hit a pothole; brown water spatters the windscreen as I drive too fast through a puddle.

'Does anyone else live up here?' Dean's read my mind.

'There's me, two women at the stables, and at the top of the lane, a farmer. He lives alone.'

'They likely to be around this time of night? Will they hear us?'

'Doubtful. People tend to keep themselves to themselves in this area.'

We're nudging into summer, so could there be poachers around at night? I've never seen one, and maybe they don't exist except in 1950s novels, but who knows?

We drive up the dirt road to the top of the logging tracks. I by-pass the small parking lot for mountain bikers, and head up the track to the left. The way is steep and riven with mud-filled fissures, but the poor old Suzuki does its best. I go as deep inwards as I can, heading for the forest's heart. A blue-black sea of slender pines surrounds us. In years to come they'll be replaced with indigenous trees, so we'll have to put the body in an area to which the loggers won't turn their attention for a good many years, where the shooting parties won't stumble upon it in the winter, and well away from the criss-crossing mountain bike paths. Grass has cannibalised the mud tracks here, and the Suzuki's wheels spin on it. I can't get stuck – we can't exactly call for a tow truck considering what we're doing here.

'We'll walk from here, Dean. Can you carry him?' *Is that you speaking Claire?*

'We can't go further in?'

'No.'

I choose a pine-covered slope at random. It's steep but will have to do.

'Should we leave the body in the car until we've dug the hole?' Dean asks.

I want to snap: 'How the fuck should I know?' The closest I've come to this kind of thing is watching *The Sopranos*. 'No,' I say instead. 'We'll take it with us, just in case someone's heard the car. We don't want them looking in the jeep and seeing it.'

My hand brushes the plastic wrapping as I reach in to grab the tools, and I'm doubly grateful that I thought to wear gloves. It's a nightmare trying to balance the tools over my shoulder while holding the torch, but my job is easy compared to Dean's.

Again I can't bear to watch him hauling the body out of the car, and when I turn he's carrying it in a fireman's lift, his knees sagging under the weight. I'm not going to offer to help. It's not just the horror of touching the body; I've got my own issues hefting the tools and trying not to trip over the branches and roots around us. There's no moon tonight, and the torch does little to cut through the blackness. The forest is a far more sinister beast at night: the trees seem to press in on us. Still, their branches shield us from the worst of the rain, which has become a deluge.

There's a yelp from behind me. Dean has fallen. Now I have no choice but to help him. I dump the tools in an area that looks suitable for a grave, and climb back up. Together we nudge the corpse down the slope using our boots. It's like rolling a heavy carpet down stairs made of dirt. Occasionally it gets snagged on a log and the tangled undergrowth. And horribly, even through my boot, the flesh beneath its covering feels hard and unforgiving.

Dean tries to say something to me, but he's too out of breath.

'I'll go first,' I say, reaching for the pickaxe. I'm not being chivalrous; if I dig, I won't be able to look at the body. My eyes keep being dragged back to it. The meagre light from our torches seems to catch on the plastic at every opportunity.

Whenever a character buries a body in the movies, they make it look easy. It's not like that in reality. Of course it isn't. I start by churning up the soil with the pickaxe. The ground is loamy and easy to move at first, but then I hit a snarl of roots. Manchee yips excitedly and hares off after a night creature. She's never yet managed to catch a rabbit or a squirrel; it's her ambition to do so. But tonight's not the night for that – the area is remote, but I can't take the risk of her drawing attention to us. I call her back, sounding too harsh, and she slinks back towards me, ears flat against her head. Her eyes are flat alien spheres in the torchlight.

Dig, dig, dig. Dean takes over for a while, prodding ineffectively at the roots with the pickaxe, but he doesn't have the stamina needed to shift them. Within seconds he's huffing like a steam train. It's up to me. The constant huff, scrape, huff dig as I shovel the clay soil away is endless, and for a while, the hole doesn't seem to be getting any bigger. I'm fitter than I've ever been, but burying a body needs more than fitness.

Three feet is all we can manage.

I turn my back while Dean rolls the body into the hole.

The sound of earth hitting plastic has an eerie finality to it, and makes the whole thing seem real. *You've buried a body in the woods, Claire. Happy now? What the* fuck *were you thinking?* I tamp it down, then gesture for Dean to help me cover it with foliage and logs.

We slog wearily up the slope back to the car. As we drive back, my headlights catch the swollen body of a badger in the undergrowth. It's the first one I've seen that isn't a furred bag of spattered guts on the side of the road.

Five

After Jamie bailed, Mae saw me through the next few months. She listened well into the early hours when I needed to vent, and had Jake over for sleepovers when I took a second job as a bartender. She encouraged me to sign up to an online dating site (which was where, years later, I'd meet Iain). She was a good friend, a lifeline. A second mother to my son.

What did I give back to her?

A place for her ex-husband to bury a body.

And then there was Zack – bright, nerdy, funny Zack, who took my surly Jake under his wing. Those years when Jake had been friendless and isolated were over. Jake was doing well at school, and the worries I'd been harbouring about him drifted away.

Jake was doing well, but I wasn't. The debts started piling up.

Mae sat me down one evening. 'You need to ask Jake's father for help, Claire.'

'But I haven't seen him in years.'

'Tell me about him. Jake never mentions him.'

Unusually for me, I'd been honest with Jake about his dad. I'd told him right from the start that Amir was little more than a sperm donor. It was an embarrassing cliché: a rich, married barrister picks up a waitress and gets her pregnant after a one-night stand. I was too proud to take anything from him until Mae told me not to be so fucking stupid.

Mae put Dean on the case. He contacted Amir and negotiated a settlement for the years he'd missed out on, plus four hundred quid a month. I steeled myself for requests for DNA tests and court battles, but it never came to that. Amir's only caveat was that we stayed out of his life. It's Amir who's paying Jake's university fees now. I still don't know if his wife knows about his son, or about me. Amir keeps our correspondence strictly minimal and impersonal, and has never once asked to meet Jake.

I gave Dean all the credit for digging me out of my financial hole, which wasn't fair. Mae was the one who'd driven the process. But here was the thing: Mae had a habit of telling me uncomfortable truths, dishing out unwanted advice and sometimes being condescending to me. And later, when Jake came out, it was Mae he told first. Not me. Not even Zack. That hurt. I've never been one of those women who prefer the company of men. I've always had female friends (although I've lost many over the years as well). But after Dean helped me out with Amir, the bond we'd created after our night of heart-to-heart drinking and talking deepened. We slid into the habit of sneaking off for coffee or a drink alone. It started when Mae went away for one of her conferences, and continued. We'd talk about everything: the boys, life, the universe, but we'd also gossip about Mae, make fun of her habit of always doing the right thing, take the piss out of her forthrightness and her work ethic. We styled ourselves as the fun parents; she was the stick-in-the-mud, the disciplinarian. I knew what I was doing. I knew this was unfair and a betrayal. And Dean was twenty years older than me – what the hell was he doing belittling his wife behind her back? There wasn't a sexual element to our connection, although I still had a schoolgirl crush on him. Truth is, he boosted my ego. He was charming and funny and entertaining, and I liked the way people looked at me with a new respect when they saw us out together.

Time passed and things got easier. I managed to secure a contract with the town's leading interior design firm, and Jake continued to do well. Dean and I continued to meet behind Mae's back.

Sometime around Christmas of the following year, Dean loaned me his car while mine was in the shop getting its MOT. It was a Lexus, an ostentatious luxury vehicle, not unlike the Merc that acted as the body's makeshift hearse. I was outside the school, waiting to pick up the boys when I found the Polaroid in the cubbyhole. It was out of focus, but it was clear enough. It showed a woman's bare brown legs, and was clearly taken while she was sitting in the passenger seat of Dean's – I recognised the leather upholstery. They weren't Mae's legs; hers were bonier. I stared at it, feeling like I'd been kicked in the gut, as if Dean was cheating on me, not Mae. Hands shaking, and feeling slightly sick, I put the photo back where I'd found it.

I had a choice: Say nothing, confront Dean, or tell Mae what I'd found.

I agonised over it. For days it was all I could think about. *Was* Dean having an affair? Why hadn't he told me? Confided in me as I confided in him? And if I'm honest, my ego was bruised: if he was in the market for an affair, why hadn't he ever tried it on with me? The next time we sneaked off for a quick pint, I blurted out that I'd found it. I tried to sound nonchalant, but came off shrill.

'Oh that,' Dean said with a shrug. 'She's just a client. I was giving her a lift and we were messing around with her camera. She'd picked up one of those vintage ones.' It slipped out smoothly and plausibly. 'Come on, Claire. You didn't think I was having an affair, did you?'

Yes.

I wanted to believe him. But deep down I knew it was a lie.

And it wasn't the only thing he was lying about.

I'm dozing on top of the duvet when I hear Manchee barking. Flushed with adrenalin, I hare down the stairs. The back door is wide open. Did I forget to shut it when we returned to the house? Oh *fuck* – is Dean still here? No. I watched him drive away at five this morning. It's now past ten.

'Helloooooo,' Sam calls.

Shite – I've forgotten we were going to walk together today.

I'm usually pleased to see Sam. She's a symbol – like Manchee, the cottage and Iain – of my New Life. My new start. Sam used to be a paramedic, but had to give it up fifteen years ago after she was almost killed in a motorbike crash. She sustained a severe head injury, which has given her aphasia, and she often has to pause to root around for the correct word. Despite this, she's relentlessly cheerful, and I've never heard her complain about anything or say a snide word about anyone. She lives in the village, in one of the converted barns. There's a cluster of them, all with sensible PVC windows and neat gardens. Her husband George is a no-nonsense ex-police officer, and seeing her now, full of smiles and normality and sunniness, I know with a numb certainty that I should have called him when I first saw the body in the boot.

Her dog Nelson barrels in and heads straight for the remaining dry pellets in Manchee's bowl. Manchee watches him in long-suffering silence.

'Sorry I'm not ready, Sam,' I say, trying to sound normal and not like someone who's been up half the night burying a corpse. 'Didn't sleep well.'

'Oh no problem. You want me to take… Right.' Sam pauses to find the word. 'You want me to take Manchee by myself?'

Be normal. Act normal. 'Nah. Give me a few and I'll come with you.'

'Have you been… Right. Digging?'

I go cold. 'What?'

'There's stuff outside. Clothes.'

Christ, I remember shrugging off my muddy gear and leaving it next to the outside table – I was far too exhausted to pack it away, but what did Dean do with his? We'd taken it in turns to shower, and I have no clue what he was up to while I was sloughing the mud off my skin. Sam may have sustained brain damage, but she's not stupid. If there are two pairs of muddy boots outside, she'll want to know why. I pad outside in bare feet, the gravel biting into my soles. *Thank God*. It's just the stuff I was using. A single glove sits next to my boots like a filthy severed hand.

'Oh yeah,' I manage. 'I was digging up by the nettle patch yesterday.' I manage a grin. 'Give me a sec and I'll get dressed.'

I race upstairs and throw on the first clothes to hand. The towels Dean and I used last night lie damply on the bathroom floor. On my way out, I scan the kitchen for other damning signs of Dean's nocturnal visit. There are two glasses next to the sink, but they blend in with the rest of the evidence of my home-alone sloth.

'Where shall we go?' Sam asks.

'Up to you.'

Manchee barks and twirls, she can overlook Nelson's thuggish behaviour if there's the chance of an outing.

We walk up the lane and Sam asks how Iain is doing. I tell her that he's back in two weeks and I can't wait to see him. This is true, but it's still an effort to sound casual.

Walk, walk, walk. I concentrate on each step to distract myself from obsessing about last night's madness. It's futile: My body is a constant reminder. My shoulders throb like rotting teeth, and there's an ache at the base of my spine as if I've been kicked there. Manchee and Nelson zoot off every so often after squirrels and rabbits. Sheep bunch in the fields next to us. The hedgerows are livid with cow parsley, and bracken is beginning its colonisation of the area, the new fronds waiting to unfurl and grasp the space around them.

Sam is telling me about one of the lonely old women she checks up on every week. Despite being registered disabled, Sam's always helping other people, doing her bit. She's one of life's good people. Sam wouldn't stab a friend in the back, or conduct a platonic affair with another woman's partner.

Sam would never bury a body in the woods.

We cut up through the woods and head along one of the side trails. A guy in a hooded raincoat emerges through the trees from the left, and for a cold second, I'm sure it's Dean.

'Helloooo,' Sam calls.

It isn't Dean of course. It's Colin. *The farmer in the dell.* He has an unusual face – lopsided, as if he's recovering from a stroke – and shrewd, deep set blue eyes. His family has been farming here for generations, and he comes across as the loneliest man I've ever met. Iain hangs out with him occasionally, but I've never said more than a couple of words to him, and all I really know about him is that he's been living alone since his father died suddenly five years ago. I don't like the way he can't seem to look me in the eye for more than a few seconds whenever we run into each other. It's not creepy exactly – I get the impression he can't quite figure me out – but it's disconcerting and shifty.

Clipper, Colin's ancient collie, comes shambling up behind him. Her skew hips are slung far lower than the rest of her body. She shies away when I touch her head. Nelson barks at her, but Manchee politely sniffs her then returns to the joys of the undergrowth and the hunt for an elusive rabbit.

Sam likes to chat, and I listen to her as she cheerfully and haltingly asks Colin about the sheep and the weather and if he wants to come to the village barbecue. I smile like a lunatic and nod along. Colin glances at me, our eyes meet fleetingly, and for a second I'm certain he knows. *He knows I buried a body in the woods.*

He mumbles his goodbyes, and when I respond seconds too late, he's already wandering on his way, raggedy collie sloping at his heels.

Sam and I continue onwards. A couple of mountain bikers hiss past on the trail that runs parallel to the logging road, making me jump. I follow my feet, listening as Sam warbles on. She's permanently upbeat. I asked her once if she was like this before the accident, but she says she can't remember. George stood by her while she went through two years of intensive rehabilitation. *In sickness and in health.* Would Iain do the same for me? Would Iain stand by me if he knew what I did last night?

I honestly don't know.

'Need to wee,' Sam says abruptly. She usually has to go at some stage during a walk.

I look up and take note of our surroundings. Oh God. We're here, at the top of rise just above the gravesite. I can make out the tracks of the Suzuki smudged in the mud. I've been so lost in my own head I haven't even noticed. And Nelson – stupid fucking Nelson – is running down into the slope in the direction of the grave. I bolt after him, Sam calling after me. Down, down I go, stumbling over discarded branches and roots. Nelson springs off in another direction, thank God, but I keep going, now desperate to see how successfully we disguised the freshly turned earth. I can make it out, but only because one of my gloves is lying next to it. I snatch it up and shove it in my pocket.

I sniff the air. More than once I've caught the stench of death while walking in the woods – that reek of spoiled, sweet meat is unmistakable. On our walks, Manchee and I have come across the severed stump of a lamb's leg, and once, the curl of a picked-clean spinal column.

There's nothing but the scent of damp earth and pine.

When I clamber back up the slope, I'm breathing hard and Sam is looking at me as if I've lost my mind.

'Sorry, Sam. I thought I saw a baby deer and I didn't want Nelson to spook it.'

Sam chuckles good-naturedly. She gets a kick out of my city-girl fascination with wildlife.

I'm feeling lighter as we walk back to the cottage. The

gravesite is well hidden, and the bracken will hopefully spring up soon and disguise it further. Sam comes in for a coffee, and we chat about the tomatoes I've recently planted in the greenhouse and her beekeeping. Village life. Country life. If you'd have told me ten years ago that I'd end up living in the middle of nowhere, ten miles from the nearest Chinese takeaway, I'd never have believed it. As we chat, I imagine Sam saying: *She seemed perfectly fine to me, officer. Surely someone who'd buried a body the night before would be jumpier?*

When she leaves, I Skype Iain. The connection is bad, the wifi is rubbish in this area, and we have one of our disjointed exchanges. I've lied to him before, but will I be able to keep a secret this rancid and poisonous? I want boredom back. For the last few weeks, since the work on the guest cottage dragged to its conclusion, I've been stultifying, occasionally day-dreaming that something would happen. Not this, though. Never this.

You don't know what you've got till it's gone.

I hose down the waterproofs I wore last night, watching the muddy water stream over the paving stones and gravel. Unable to settle, I circle the cottage. It usually comforts me, but not today. We moved here on impulse. The plan was to find somewhere nearer to Iain's parents in Scotland, but when we saw the ad for the cottage on Rightmove – a 'fixer-upper in an idyllic location' – we fell in love with its stone walls, the acre of land, and the huge ancient oak tree that spreads its limbs over the property as if protecting it. The cottage instantly reminded me of Dean and Mae's Victorian terrace, the house I'd longed for all those years ago. Not in looks exactly, but the vibe was similar: an old place, bursting with character. Moving here has meant a completely fresh start, and a new way of life for me. There are no jobs in the area, so until we start getting an income from the rental cottage I'm basically living off Iain. So far, I've managed to live with the guilt of not paying my own way. But it's the garden that's really been a revelation. I've never had one before, and I'm learning as I go, helped along by YouTube videos and Google. The plan is to grow our own vegetables, maybe get some chickens – go the whole lentil-eating nine yards. I'm not sure if I'll ever go that far, but I'm beginning to love the garden as much as I love the woods.

Manchee at my heels as usual, I head to the back of the property and the guest cottage. All that's left to do is install the bathroom fittings, paint the kitchen, and furnish it. I stick my head in the door and breathe in the clean smell of fresh plaster. Dean's words come back to me: '*Mae always said you'd be suited to fixing up an old place with a scarf around your hair.*'

Unsettled again, next I make for the giant nettle patch that lurks shaggily behind the guest cottage. This is one of my major projects. I've got a half-baked plan to clear it and create a vegetable patch here. I snatch at one of the taller plants without thinking. I'm not wearing gloves, and the leaves sting my palms. Part of me wants the pain. *You deserve the pain.* I pull out another, then another, enjoying the faint ripping sound as their interconnected roots are prised from the soil. In the distance, I can make out the whir and chug of Colin's tractor.

The sting in my palms has become a low throb: a constant pins and needles tingle, like the onslaught of the world's longest panic attack.

Six

Everything fell apart a few months after Jake's thirteenth birthday.

I'd taken the kids to see one of the X-Men films as a post-exam treat, and I could hear Mae's voice the second I pulled up outside their house. She was screaming at someone – Dean, presumably. I told the kids to stay in the car.

'Shit', Jake whispered.

I didn't tell him off for swearing. All I could think was that Mae had discovered the truth about Polaroid Girl. Selfishly, I started to fret that Dean might reveal that I knew about her, too, or maybe Mae had found out about our occasional private jaunts. Mae came storming out of the house just as I was about to knock on the door. She dragged me along the pavement and out of earshot of the boys. Their anxious faces watched us through the windscreen. 'He's bankrupted us, Claire,' she said. She was shaking. I'd never seen her anywhere near this rattled. 'He's done it again.' Then it all came out: Dean hadn't been paying the mortgage on the house, he owed thousands on the Lexus (which he'd leased) and he was about to be investigated for a bout of 'creative accounting'. And it wasn't the first time – it was why they'd left London.

I hadn't seen it coming. Sure, Dean never seemed to do any work – he was always available to collect the boys and hang out with me, but I'd assumed that was because he was self-employed, and worked when it suited him. And he always seemed to have money. He always paid for everything and spoiled Zack and Jake rotten. I knew there was no way they could maintain their lifestyle on Mae's academic salary alone.

'Why didn't you tell me this before, Mae?' I asked.

'Didn't want to worry you. You have enough to deal with being a single mom.'

The shame came then. *You are such a two-faced bitch, Claire.* 'What can I do?'

'You can help me pack. Zack and I are moving back to London.'

It's been a week since we buried him.

Already the brambles are poking exploratory fingers towards the balding patch where I ripped up the nettles. Elsewhere, the bluebells have gone, sucked back invisibly into the earth and replaced by foxgloves. This happens so fast and seamlessly it's almost as if an invisible gardener has been snooping around at night. Last year I'd thought the foxgloves beautiful, a row of bright soldiers. Now there's something aggressive about their spears of bright purple. Their other, more menacing names – digitalis, witches fingers – seem to suit them. In the woods behind the house, the bracken is creeping in, an unstoppable green tide.

I can't shake the sense that something has shifted in the garden, as if it's moved into a new, grimmer biosphere. There are fewer flowers than there were last year when we moved in, I'm sure of it, and some kind of blackish mould is creeping over the concrete slabs that snake up through the garden towards the guest cottage. Still, the tomatoes I planted in the greenhouse are coming to life. That's something.

Yesterday, Sam came over to ask me if I'd look after Nelson for the night as she and George have to stay over in Hereford so that she's in time for her 'fit to work' assessment. Nelson is a different animal today. He's subdued, as if staying here is a punishment. I cook liver for him and Manchee, shiny slabs of glistening offal, slimy and porous. I've been careless with the packaging, and blood pools on the counter and drips down the kitchen cupboards.

Iain will be home in less than a week. I'm nowhere near where I wanted to be in the schedule. Hours go by where I do nothing but watch the bees haze around in the lavender outside the kitchen window. They're sluggish and die easily, and there's a graveyard of them lying on their backs on the window ledge. At least I managed to finish painting the guest cottage's kitchen, although I'm not happy with the result. It's a lime green that's supposed to echo the garden and bring the outside in, but it actually gives the place a cheap, primary school aura. I wanted to have cleared the nettle patch before Iain returned and sand down the old bed that's also going in the cottage, but since Corpse Night I haven't been sleeping. Last night I stayed up watching old episodes of the *X Files* until the light came up.

Manchee wolfs her food before Nelson can snaffle it, then pads around my feet on high alert. She hasn't been for a walk yet, and I didn't go yesterday, so she's watching every move I make.

I have no energy, but I haul on my boots and collect the dogs' leads. Nelson perks up.

I walk up the road towards the wood at the top.

I know what I'm doing. It's poking a rotten tooth with a tongue. Tempting fate.

I scramble down the slope, trying not to think about how the plastic-wrapped body slithered down here in the mud. I circle the area where it lies. The logs we rolled over the spot look flimsier and more artificially placed than the last time I was here.

I call Manchee to me. She approaches warily, ears flat, as if

I'm about to hit her. I've never hit her. I grab her collar and position her directly over where the body lies, waiting to see if she's interested. She shakes free and bounds after Nelson, who's spotted a squirrel.

The dogs don't seem able to detect the stench of death. That has to be good, right? Hopefully that means that foxes won't dig it up.

Relieved, I head home.

On the way back, a pheasant explodes out of the undergrowth and I scream.

In the end, Mae decided not to return to London and managed to keep the house. It was Dean who was forced to move away.

Mae still didn't know about my and Dean's secret meetings. Twisted with guilt, I was determined to make it up to her, and I did at first, more than pulling my weight with the boys, and trying to be a good listener and a solid shoulder. I vowed that this time I'd take her side and not Dean's. She told me everything. How Dean had been flying by the seat of his pants business-wise, hooking up with dodgy clients and taking financial risks. Once again, Dean had only received a slap on the wrist for his 'creative accounting,' but to her credit, as far as I knew, Mae never bad-mouthed Dean to Zack.

I missed my and Dean's liaisons more than I wanted to admit. With a hole in my life to fill, I followed Mae's advice, and threw myself back into the murky waters of online dating. That's when I met Iain, a gruff, no nonsense Scot who worked in security. He couldn't have been more different to Dean – or Jamie. Iain worked away a lot, but things got serious pretty quickly.

The text from Dean came out of the blue: 'Fancy a few pints?' He was back in the area visiting Zack. The old excitement at the thought of seeing him surfaced. I was supposed to be meeting Iain that night, but I cancelled, telling him I thought I was coming down with the flu. Zack and Jake would be out at a party, so I'd have the flat to myself. I invited Dean to visit me at home – something I hadn't done before.

Fate intervened. Jake fell violently ill at the party with food poisoning, and unable to get hold of me, called Mae. When she dropped him off, she recognised Dean's leased Lexus in the driveway. I made up some crap about Dean 'just dropping by' to return something Jake had left in his car, but she knew I was lying. She didn't say anything that night, or make a scene. But the next day she sent me a one-line email: 'He's never going to sleep with you, you dumb bitch.'

Seven

Three a.m.

He answers on my fifth attempt. 'You shouldn't call me, Claire.' I can hear from the lag in his voice that he's been sleeping. *How dare he sleep when I can't!*

'I have to know, Dean.' Silence. 'I have to know if you killed him.' *I want to go to the police. I can't live like this.* 'I have to know who he is.'

He sighs. 'Not over the phone.'

'I need to know *now*.' Again he doesn't answer me. '*Dean.* Fucking answer me!'

'Meet me tomorrow.'

'Where?'

'London. Euston Station.'

'I'm not coming all the way to London!'

'Halfway, then. Where would that be?'

'Um... God. Crewe, probably.'

'What time?'

'Three?'

'Fine. I'll meet you outside the entrance.'

He hangs up.

The train is packed. I've pre-booked a ticket but there's a woman with a kid on her lap in my seat. I sit outside the lavatory, my stomach churning.

Dean is ten minutes late.

'Not here,' he says before I say a word. I follow him into a Costa outlet on one of the platforms. It's nestled between a waiting area and a grimy pub. I want a drink. I want a whole bottle of vodka. I order a latte.

We sit at a corner table. 'Tell me, Dean. Tell me everything.'

He sighs. 'Can I trust you, Claire?'

I snort. 'You trusted me to help you bury a body no questions asked, so yeah. I'd say you can.'

'Zack's got himself into trouble.'

'What kind of trouble?' *Body in the trunk kind of trouble, idiot.*

'He's... He started messing around with drugs. Hard drugs. He got in with a rough crowd.'

Zack? This doesn't sound like the Zack I know. The little boy who stood up for my little boy. Not *my* Zack. 'Dean, are you saying that *Zack* killed the man in the boot?'

'No! Not intentionally. The... the guy, he caused a lot of trouble for Zack. Threatened him with violence. Got him hooked on drugs. He was a monster, Claire. He was killing my boy.'

'How did he die?'

'The fella attacked Zack, he fought back, the guy fell, hit his head. They were both wasted. It was an accident, Claire.'

'Then you *have* to go to the cops.'

'You don't get it. This won't be Zack's first brush with the law. What if they don't believe his story?'

'The autopsy will prove it, Dean.' For some reason I'm picturing my lounge full of cops – a mixture of the archetypes from detective dramas: Courageous, flawed women and hard-nosed drunks who secretly have hearts of gold.

'It's too late. We buried him.'

'It's not too late, Dean. Think about it. It was just a moment of madness. We panicked.'

'Zack won't survive prison, Claire. Like I said, he's had some problems recently.'

I haven't spoken to Zack for months. Not since he fell out with Jake. I don't know why they fell out, and Jake won't say. *It happens*, Iain had said, counselling me not to interfere. 'Yeah, you said. Problems with drugs, right?'

'Not just that. Depression as well. Zack tried to… kill himself.'

'Jesus. When?'

'Three months ago.'

'Why didn't you tell me this before?'

'We lost touch.'

This is true. My fault – I could have done more.

'Zack called me earlier that evening. Asked me to help him. I couldn't say no, could I, Claire? He's my son for the love of God. And after Mae and I…'

'Where's Zack now?'

'I told him to lie low. I'm getting him help.'

'But… won't someone report the… the' – I search for the right word: *the man, the corpse, the body* – 'won't someone report the drug dealer missing?'

'Doubtful. People like that, they come and go all the time. Itinerant.'

'Where did this happen?'

'You don't need to know the details, Claire.'

'Don't tell me what I need to know,' I hiss. Two men in blue suits glance over at us.

'All you need to know is that the bloke won't be reported missing. There's nothing to worry about. It's all going to work out.'

'What about CCTV?'

'Huh?'

'You must have manoeuvred him into the car somehow,

Dean. What if they've caught you on camera?'

He places his hand over mine. Once, this would have given me a thrill, now it fills me with revulsion. 'Claire... that's not going to happen. It's all going to be okay, I promise.'

Eight

I'm ten minutes early to collect Iain from the station. I park, then sit back in my seat. I haven't slept again. Dean's Zack-in-extremis story isn't sitting right with me. I should be relieved to have an explanation, and one that helps alleviate the guilt. I owe Zack. I want to protect him.

Lost in thought again, I jump as Iain taps on the window. Manchee goes crazy when she sees him and tries to leap over the front seat. As Iain squeezes me in a bear hug and kisses me, I pull away too soon. His mouth is sour, and tastes of plane food.

I thought having him back would make everything instantly okay. It doesn't.

'Tell me everything,' he says as I ease into the traffic.

I buried a body in the woods. 'I've painted the cottage.' *I buried a body in the woods.* 'I've almost cleared the nettle patch.' *I buried a body in the woods.* 'Oh, and I planted some tomatoes.'

'Sounds exciting,' he says in his wry Edinburgh accent. Both he and Dean are originally from Scotland, and I naively thought this might bring them together, but on the first and only occasion they met, it was loathing at first sight.

I half-listen to him on the drive home, groggy from lack of

sleep, I need all my concentration to stay alert and not drive into a hedgerow. He hates the expats he's forced to hang out with in Qatar, and he fills me in on the gossip. 'They want me to do one more contract, Claire. What do you think?'

'When?'

'Soon. Couple of weeks.'

Don't leave me. Don't leave me alone with the body in the woods. 'That soon?'

'Aye, but the money will be good. Enough to see us through for a long while. Two years at least.'

'Let's talk about it when you've had a rest. You must be exhausted.'

'I missed you,' he says.

'Me too.' And I have. Dean would never have pitched up at the house if Iain were at home. Iain. Solid, dependable Iain. *You'll get bored*, Dean had warned me after they met. But I haven't got bored. Not yet. Iain, like the house, Manchee, the garden, my friendship with Sam, is my shot at redemption.

While Iain showers, I head out to water the tomatoes in the greenhouse. I've been overfeeding them, and they've already started to spread. *Feed me, Seymour.* There's a new, festering peaty odour in the air that I'm pretty sure isn't normal.

I resist the urge to head up to the nettle patch and yank some more out of the earth. The lumps from my last lot of stings are still itchy.

There are voices coming from downstairs: I can make out Iain's low burr and the rumble of another male. He's been back home now for two days. We haven't yet fallen into our easy camaraderie, but it usually takes a few days until we readjust. I've been trying to hide my exhaustion, and before I head downstairs I dab concealer around my eyes.

I greet Colin as politely as someone with severe insomnia can, and ask him about Clipper. He grumbles something unintelligible while he stares at a spot above my head. He appears to like Iain, though. They move on to a discussion about the best place to get Iain's chainsaw serviced, and I excuse myself and head upstairs to the computer. I've been buying stuff online for the holiday cottage, in the hopes that some retail therapy might help numb the stress. It hasn't. In the next couple of days I'll take photos of the guest cottage and put them up on AirBnB. I've been looking forward to this part for months, but now it seems like a pointless chore. Also open on my browser is a website listing the U.K's missing people, and for the last couple of days I've been obsessively scrolling through the photos of men. There are more than I expected. I've been trying to estimate the size of the man to narrow down the field, but I only have a vague sense of him being well under six foot and slender.

Then there's what Dean said about Zack. *If that's true, it's unlikely the man will be reported missing.*

I text Jake and ask him if he's free to chat. He's got his own life now, and I've lost count of the number of times he's promised to call me and hasn't. But this time he texts back straight away with a: 'oh hey mom sure.' We trade updates, and then I drop it into conversation. 'You heard from Zack?'

'Huh? No. Not for ages.'

Does Jake know his best friend tried to kill himself? I'll have to tread carefully. 'How come you two fell out anyway?'

A sigh. 'Really, Mom? You want to do this now?'

'Yes.'

'Christ, okay. Hold on.' I hear him light something and inhale. Could be a fag, could be a joint. 'It was about Thailand if you must know.'

'What about Thailand?'

'Well, like a while ago we were both pissed off with our courses. He said he was going to drop out and go travelling for a bit, and I kind of said I might join him.'

'You *what?*'

'Don't freak out. I didn't drop out, did I? Hold on.' I hear him hissing at someone that he'll be there 'in a sec.' A new boyfriend? Is this sporadic contact with someone I used to spend all day with normal? Is this my fault too?

'And Zack's okay as far as you know?' I ask.

'Yeah. He's totally loving Thailand.'

'Wait – he's still there?'

Another sigh. 'Yeah. Six months now. He's having a great time far as I can tell.'

'You know this for sure?'

'What's with all the questions?'

'Just curious. I... I had a bad dream about him.'

He laughs. 'Jesus, Mom, seriously?'

'Seriously.'

'Look, he's doing great. His Facebook's been dead, but a mutual mate went out to see him a couple of weeks ago so I got the intel. He's working out there, hooked up with some American girl, and it looks like he might stay longer.'

'And you're sure he's been out there for six months?'

'Yeah. At least.'

'And he hasn't come home once?'

'Not as far as I know. Mom, have you been drinking or something?'

I don't answer straight away. All I can think is: Zack couldn't have been involved in the death of whoever we buried in the woods.

Dean was lying to me.

Nine

I call Dean the second Iain leaves the cottage to finish varnishing the guest cottage's windows – the last job on the list. His mobile keeps going to voice mail, but I don't give up. He answers on the tenth try. I don't greet him. All I say is, 'Three, Crewe, tomorrow, be there or else,' then hang up, my heart thudding.

It's warm again today, and I wander outside to find Manchee. I haven't seen her for an hour or so, which is unusual as she's my shadow (and a partner in crime – a witness). She's lying on the grass underneath the sprawling oak tree, and there's something grey and furry between her paws. Has she finally caught a rabbit?

She looks up at me almost guiltily as I approach. Then I catch a glimpse of its long bald tail. It's a rat, and it appears to be missing its head. My stomach flips.

I back away.

'Hey!' Iain calls. I whirl around. 'Thought you said you'd cleared the nettle patch?' he says this good-naturedly.

'I did.'

I jog over to the area behind the guest cottage. The nettles are back. But that's impossible. Isn't it? Mind befuddled by lack of sleep, I must have pulled out fewer plants than I thought.

It's the only explanation I can think of.

I make up a half-hearted lie about heading to Cardiff to buy kitchen sundries for the guest cottage. Iain offers to come with me, but I airily tell him he'll only get bored. It's not much of a betrayal compared to what I've already done, but still – I can't help thinking: *this is where the rot sets in.*

I get a seat on the train to Crewe this time. My mind keeps straying to the garden. It didn't behave like this last year. It isn't just the tenacious nettle patch or the relative lack of flowering plants. The black mould that has started to encroach over the garden slabs is getting worse, taking on a tar-like quality. The magnolia bush isn't budding, and the tea roses the previous owners planted are shrivelled and sick. It could be because I'm inept and haven't got a clue that I'm doing. But then again...

As the train rattles its way into the station, I scratch at my palms. I've been pulling at the nettles again and they're red and lumped with stings.

This time Dean is early and is waiting for me at 'our' table in the Costa outlet. I'm too tired and weak to vent my fury at him. I'm continually nauseous. All I seem able to stomach is bread. Sliced white bread which turns claggy in my mouth.

He's as smart as ever in a slick grey suit and red tie, as if he's on his way to a business meeting. People are shooting him surreptitious glances as if he's a celebrity they're trying to place. *Bastard.* I know my hair is tangled and greasy and my shirt is wrinkled and smells stale. I'm absorbing all the stress for both of us like a scruffy version of Dorian Gray's portrait.

'Zack's in Thailand, Dean,' I say as I sit opposite him. The table is sticky and peppered with old sugar wrappers – why am I noticing details like this?

'You want a coffee?' he asks casually, as if we're just two old acquaintances catching up.

The anger comes then. 'No I don't want a fucking coffee.

Did you hear what I just said?'

'Keep your voice down.' He says this flatly, like a threat. I find myself looking at his hands, imagining them wrapped around someone's neck. I never knew the real Dean. I was fooled and charmed by him all those years ago. It makes me feel weak and stupid. It's my own fault.

'You made me bury a body. You *made* me.'

'I didn't make you do anything, Claire.' He softens his voice. 'There's stuff you don't know about me.'

'No shit.'

A roll of the eyes as if I'm an exasperating teenager. 'Do you want me to tell you or not?'

He's ruined my life, poisoned my home. Of course I want to know what I've done. Of course I want to know who I buried in my woods. 'Go on.'

'I have a secret life.'

I immediately think about the girl in the Polaroid, and along with the thought comes an old spike of jealousy that I truly hate myself for. 'Girlfriends you mean.'

'No. Not that. I bait and trap people online.'

'*What?*' I almost laugh. 'What the fuck are you talking about?'

'The man we buried was a paedophile.'

Now I do laugh. The people around us who were staring at Dean are now staring at me.

'I'm serious, Claire.'

'Yeah right. You're saying you're some kind of online vigilante?'

'The guy we buried got out of prison and tried to go after a little girl. We baited him. Things got ugly.'

'We?'

'There's a group of us. It's what we do.'

Jesus. 'Okay. I'll bite. So this paedophile you baited, how come he hasn't been reported missing?'

'Who says he hasn't?'

'I don't believe you, Dean. You're talking shite.'

He shrugs and then gives me a small smile. 'I wouldn't have got you involved in this if I could help it, Claire.'

Another lie. He's not even bothering to elaborate, or make it sound reasonable. He sips his coffee nonchalantly. Another shrug: *Believe what you want.*

Have I got a choice?

He gets up abruptly and leaves without saying goodbye.

I helped Dean because I owed him. I owed him – and Mae – for helping Jake and me all those years ago. I owed him for sorting out the cash from Amir, for being my friend.

I'm tired of reminiscing. I can't go back. I have to go forward. There's nothing else in my past to pick over.

There's one thing.

It shouldn't have happened. I'm not an alcoholic. I've never woken up and longed for a glug of vodka. But shortly after Iain moved in with me and started talking about making our relationship permanent, for a while it became a habit to have a few shots or glasses of wine every evening, and occasionally during my lunch break.

Things were made worse by the fact that Jake had pulled away from me. Really, I should have been relieved that my once anxious son was exerting his independence, but still. It hurt. Being one of the few openly gay kids at school had its perks, and Jake had collected an entourage of confident, chatty girls. He and Zack still hung out, albeit not as often as before.

I saw Dean less and less regularly (and always behind Iain's back – old habits die hard). Then I heard via Jake that Mae had gone to the U.S for several months and Dean had moved back home to be there for Zack. I hadn't spoken to Mae since she sent that barbed email. Occasionally I'd spot her around town, and we had an unspoken agreement to pretend we hadn't seen each other. As the boys now did their own thing and didn't need fetching and carrying, there was no need for us to have contact.

When it happened, I'd had a difficult day: A client who'd decided at the last minute to change the colour of the kitchen cupboards I was customising for her. I'd already bought the paint, and she was refusing to refund me. To take the edge off, after work I sat in the van and helped myself to the half-jack of vodka I kept in the console.

The client lived in a rural area, and by the time I left for home, it was getting dark. I drove carefully along the unfamiliar country roads, trying to shake off the stress of the day. It happened in a split second. I heard my phone beep – Jake had sent me a text – and I took my eyes off the road for an instant. The next thing I knew, the van was nose-first in a field. I'd missed a sharp S-bend and ploughed through a hedge. The van's airbags didn't deploy, but I'd worn my seatbelt and although shocked, I was unhurt.

Then the real implications of what I'd done came trickling in. I was over the limit. If a passing car stopped to help, they'd probably call the police. I'd be breathalysed. At the very least I'd lose my licence and my livelihood, and the insurance wouldn't pay out. Fortunately, the van was partially hidden from passing traffic, so I had a chance to get out of the situation before the cops were called.

It didn't even occur to me to call Iain for help. I knew him too well. He had – *has* – too much integrity to attempt a cover-up, and I didn't want him to know about my secret boozing.

So I called Dean. He came immediately. He parked his Lexus down a narrow lane within walking distance of the crash site, handed me the keys and told me to get out of there. Dean told the cops that I'd loaned him the van so that he could move some furniture, and had run off the road when he swerved to avoid a fox.

Thanks to Dean I got away with it. And he did it no questions asked.

Ten

The rot in the garden is getting worse. There are now small pockets of mulchy, foul-smelling earth in amongst the beds, as if the land is softly rotting from the inside. Iain says the mould on the steps is perfectly natural (despite the fact that we're having a dry summer). I've tried washing it off with the power-hose, but within hours it's back.

I'm still not sleeping. I've got into the habit of lying next to Iain, waiting until I'm certain he's fast asleep, and then creeping into the spare room where I keep the laptop. I spend hours watching documentaries on YouTube about body farms. I Google 'decomposition'. There is nothing I don't know about post-mortem insect activity. The same old sad faces look back at me when I trawl the missing person sites. And, surprise, surprise, no kiddie fiddlers have been reported missing.

I uploaded the photos of the cottage yesterday, and this evening, a message from AirBnb is waiting in my inbox. My first booking. I reply to the enquiry with an ebullience I don't feel. Iain leaves for Doha again soon, and I'll be on my own. I'm not sure if I'm relieved about this or not. I think I am, and I think Iain is – the lack of sleep is making me both irritable and spacey.

The small room's walls seem to close in on me.

I pad downstairs, careful not to wake Iain, and head outside. Manchee joins me. She doesn't bark or hare off into the night, but sticks to my side as if we're co-conspirators. We dodge the sensor lights and head to the back of the property.

There's no ambient light and the stars are out. I sit under the huge oak tree that spreads its huge arms across our piece of land, and dig my fingers into the earth.

When the worst happens it comes out of the blue.

I'm moping around the kitchen, making a cup of lemon tea I don't really want. My first guests arrived three days after Iain left for Doha, and I'm already heartily sick of them. They're elderly, big walkers, posh, and are always knocking tentatively on the kitchen door and asking for things or advice on walking routes. They're clearly the type of people who make sure they get their money's worth; the equivalent of tourists who stuff themselves at the hotel buffet even though they never normally eat breakfast.

This is your future, Claire. You wanted this.

I'm trying to figure out if I miss Iain but, if I'm honest, not having to hide my exhaustion is a relief. It's becoming so pervasive that it's affecting my vision. Some days I feel as if I'm viewing the world through a narrow tunnel.

Manchee has picked up on my lethargy, and lies on the kitchen floor, her head flopped between her paws in the universal sign of dog dejection. Her ears prick up and she barks. The guests are out for an early morning stroll, an enterprise that has taken hours of preparation, and I assume it's them returning, probably to complain about the grass being too wet or something.

It's not the guests.

Sam is standing outside the door. She's holding something in her left hand, wrapped in the cagoule she always takes with her for her walks. Nelson is panting hard and he doesn't attempt to barge in and scoff Manchee's remaining food.

'Claire,' Sam says. 'Right. I need... phone.'

I've never seen Sam like this – ruffled and jumpy. It's a fifteen-minute walk to her house from my place, so why would she need the phone? There's no mobile network reception in this area, but still. I want to believe that she's come across an injured mountain biker and she needs to call an ambulance, but my eyes keep straying to the cagoule. She's holding it stiffly – away from her body.

I don't want to ask her what's happened, but it'll look weird if I don't. 'Are you okay, Sam?'

'Fine. Need to call... Need to call George. Found something. Right. In the woods.'

'What?'

'It's a... Right.'

It takes her longer than usual to find the word. *C'mon, c'mon, c'mon.*

'It's a... Right. Jaw.'

I stand at the top of the driveway and watch as the SOCO vans and police cars whizz past, heading up towards the woods. The day has turned into an unusually hot one, a scorcher, and sweat dribbles down my sides.

'Helloooo!' Sam is walking along in their wake, her husband George at her side. They join me at the top of the driveway.

'So what do you think about all this palaver?' George huffs at me. His face is slimed with sweat. He's a cockney, as round as a ball, and wheezes every so often. 'Seems like some bugger's been dumping body parts in our woods.'

'It's... Right. Exciting,' Sam says. She's enjoying this – they both are. Nelson isn't with her for once. Bloody *bloody* Nelson. He was the one who'd found the jawbone, crunching it between his strong Labrador teeth. And as an ex-paramedic, Sam knew immediately that the bone in her dog's jaws was human.

The foxes must have dug up the body after all.

'Where were you when Nelson found the... part, Sam?' I haven't had a chance to ask this yet. She struggles to describe it, and George takes over. It sounds like she was a fair distance from the gravesite when she noticed what was clamped between her dog's jaws.

Could foxes have scattered the parts that far from the gravesite?

It's possible, isn't it?

Or... Could there be another body in the woods? A body that isn't mine?

Ridiculous.

But still. There's a kernel of hope. Dean was right. This area, with its thousands of acres of neglected woodland, is the ideal place to dump a corpse. It's perfectly possible that someone else had the same idea. I desperately want to walk to the gravesite and check it out, but this is out of the question. By now, the police and their dogs will be scouring the scene, and the last thing I should do is draw attention to it.

'Don't look so shook up, girl,' George says to me.

'Will they want to talk to all of us? The police I mean.' *They'll come. They'll come, all right. What are you going to say?*

'Course.' George laughs. 'Worried are you? Got something to hide?'

I manage a watery smile. 'Just some bad wiring up in the cottage there.' *Ha bloody ha.* 'Have they told you anything?' I ask him. As an ex-cop, they might have shared information with him.

'Nah. Just that whoever dumped her probably did so fairly recently.'

I stare at him. 'Dumped *her?*'

'Yeah.'

'The jaw belonged to a woman?'

'It's usually a woman, love. These cases.' George sighs. 'Sick bastard whoever it is. Look, I know Iain's away. You want to stay with us till this all blows over?'

'Oh that's kind. But I'm fine.'

'You're not… Right. Worried, Claire?' Sam asks.

'No. I don't get scared.' It's almost true. *People who dispose of bodies in the woods have no right to be scared.*

A West Mercia police car stops next to us. A young red-faced man in a short-sleeved shirt and a stab vest gets out. He asks us to refrain from walking in the woods and says that someone will be along soon to take a statement from us all.

I ask George and Sam if they want to come in for a cup of tea. I don't really want company – the elderly guests will no doubt be back soon – but George says they'd best head home in case the police arrive to talk to them again.

When I reach the back door, the couple are waiting for me. They tell me that they ran into the police during their ramble, and they're clearly bewildered to find themselves in the middle of so much action. To their credit, they don't treat it with salacious glee, but are wide-eyed with fear as if they expect to be the next victims. 'We've decided to go back home,' the man says. His wife shoots me a faintly aggrieved glance, as if the corpse in the woods is a stunt I've cooked up to fuck up their walking holiday.

If only they knew.

I see them off, then collect a pile of clean sheets and head dutifully to the guest cottage. It's spotless: the linen folded passive aggressively on the bed, the mugs upended on the draining board. It's cleaner than when they arrived. I flop down on the bed and stare up at the ceiling. The beams I stained black to add to the bedroom's country chic ambiance are dotted with white spider egg sacs. Manchee jumps up and lies next to me guiltily. She knows she's not supposed to be on the bed, but sod it. I shut my eyes.

Manchee woofs and leaps off the bed. I sit up. How long have I been out? I wipe my hands across my face. The room is dimmer than it was, and the light has taken on the golden hue of early evening. I must have been out for hours. Good. I needed it.

There's a knock on the door. I run my fingers through my hair and shout that I'm on my way. I'm expecting to see Sam and Nelson, but there's a stranger – a middle-aged woman dressed in jeans a sweat-stained blue shirt – hovering outside.

'Sorry to startle you.' She introduces herself as D.C Morgan and asks if I'm the owner of the property. 'Went to the main residence but no one was there,' she says. 'Mind if I have a word?'

Manchee jumps up at her and I grab the dog's collar as an excuse to hide my face while I get my expression under control. 'Of course. Let's head back to the cottage.'

Perversely, rather than being flooded by fear, I'm actually crackling with energy. *Here we go.* I've played this scene over and over in my head, but I didn't expect to feel like this. Shards of heat – not ice – run up and down my spine. My hands, lumped with their nettle stings, tingle almost pleasantly.

'Wild round here, isn't it?' the policewoman says as we head down the path. The black mould sucks at the soles of my boots. The woman doesn't seem to notice it, or if she does, she doesn't mention it. 'Must take a lot of upkeep.'

You have no idea. 'Oh it does.' I grin ruefully. 'Didn't really think about what I was taking on.'

'You moved here only recently then?'

'A year ago or so.' I explain about Iain working away. 'Will you need to talk to him too?'

'Yeah. If you give me his details I'll get someone to call him.'

I offer her a cup of tea, but she declines. She sounds vaguely northern. I find myself babbling about the area, and the work it took to fix up the guest cottage. I make the renovation sound like a Herculean task. Despite the danger of the situation, for some reason it's important to me that this woman doesn't judge me for not having a career.

Then we get into it.

'You walk a lot in the woods?' she asks.

'Yes. Almost every day.'

'And have you seen anything you might term suspicious?'

'No. Never.'

'No one strange, a vehicle you might not have recognised?'

'Well, the woods can get busy during the weekend with the mountain bikers.'

She looks around. 'Quiet here. You don't get lonely?'

'No. I like it.'

'I'm a city girl myself. Never been one for the outdoors.'

'Me too. Not now, I mean. But before.' We share a smile. 'Do they… Are they getting any closer to identifying it? The body, I mean. A friend of mine found the jawbone.'

The smile flits away. 'Not yet. Not sure what we're dealing with at the mo. Can't tell you much more.'

George is right. It's a woman.

I discover this from the Sky news banner scrolling at the bottom of the TV screen: 'Body of a woman discovered in Morton-on-Spay woods'. There's an aerial shot of the area, showing the woods – my woods – and the occasional Monopoly piece sized house on its outskirts. The area looks wilder and more sparsely inhabited from above. I can't make out the gravesite; the foliage is too thick, so there's still a thread of hope that this isn't *my* body. Because there are two choices here: the body I buried was that of a woman, or there are two bodies in the woods. Mine and this one. But what are the fucking chances of that?

It's horrible to think that I'd rather there was a serial killer out there dumping bodies in the vicinity than the police or Iain or *anyone* discovering what I've done.

And if it *is* my body, then this is yet another betrayal from Dean. I buried a woman in the woods. Why does this feel more shocking than when I thought the corpse was a man?

Mae. I betrayed Mae.

Did I bury her, too?

No.

Why did Dean let me think it was a man?

Mae. Because it's Mae. He wanted to throw you off.

No. I can't think like that. The only way to be sure is to go to the gravesite and see if it's been disturbed.

You can't do that.

There's no reason to believe it's Mae. Why would Dean kill her? Their divorce wasn't exactly amicable, but it was fair. And Zack's too old to be a pawn in any power struggles they might be having. *Maybe he had a life insurance policy on her – some more creative accounting perhaps, policies in her name.*

Now panicked, I try to log onto her Facebook account. She blocked me ages ago and, in any case, it looks like she's left the site. I run upstairs and dig out my old mobile, the only place her number is stored. The battery is dead, and while I wait for it to charge I refresh the *Guardian* website, I scan through the *Daily Mail*, I Google 'body Morton woods'. There are nuggets of fresh information, but nothing to set my mind at ease. Possibilities that it could be a missing teen are dismissed, and apparently they've found more pieces of the skull, as well as a thighbone.

There's no mention of plastic sheeting or suspicious tyre tracks.

Stop being paranoid.

Phone charged, I call Mae's number.

It's no longer in use.

Don't panic. Mae isn't the sort of person who won't be missed.

It's dark outside, but the garden beckons. I collect a flashlight, and Manchee and I head outside for one of our nightly sojourns. She's getting used to them now, and seems to enjoy them. First I check on the nettle patch, my Sisyphean task. Some part of my mind insists that if I eradicate the weeds then the poison will be gone from this place. They look less insidious at night, smaller, almost friendly. The oak tree's branches cast shadows around me, but I'm not frightened of the dark any more. There are worse things to fear. Next I check on the runner beans. Snails have attacked them and their leaves are little more than fragments. And in the greenhouse, several of my tomatoes have split and burst – the overripe fruit spilling juice and seeds over the floor. Many of the plants' leaves are scrolled up like arthritic fingers. A nasty white fungus has grown over some of their stalks.

The poison is spreading.

Eleven

I know from Sam's uncharacteristic hesitant knock on the door that she has something unpleasant to tell me. I've been trying and failing to nap on the couch. Last night I didn't even bother going back to bed; I knew it would be fruitless. I've travelled through exhaustion and reached a place where colours are brighter, smells are dimmer and I almost feel manic rather than wiped out. 'They've…. Right. Arrested Colin. Taken him in for questioning.'

My numb brain fights to digest what she's just said. 'Why Colin?'

'He's got a… you know.'

'A what?'

'A… Right. A wife.'

'Colin has a *wife*? But I thought he lived alone? And in any case, why does that –'

'He did have one. She… Right. Disappeared. Long time ago before me and George came here. Fifteen years ago.'

'Hang on. So the police think that the body might be Colin's wife's remains?' *It might not be my body, it might not be the body Dean and I buried in the woods.* Perhaps my body was a man after all – hell, perhaps the preposterous paedo story is even true. That means Mae is safe. 'So the remains they found have been buried for fifteen years?'

'No. Right,' Sam is saying. 'Freezer.'

'What?'

'Freezer. George thinks he might have stored her in the freezer. Then... Right. Decided to get rid of her recently. That'd why... Right. They think it could be her.'

'Why would Colin do that?'

'Right. Freezer broke maybe. Smell.'

'Who told you about his wife?'

'Um... Colin's friend. The man, the man at the cottage, next to the church. Oh bugger, what's his name? Fat. White dog.'

I know who she's talking about, but I can't unearth his name either. I'm on nodding terms with him. He's unkempt and morbidly obese, but in contrast his dog, some kind of miniature poodle, is manicured to within an inch of its life.

'Are you... Right. Coming to the barbecue this afternoon? Five p.m.'

I'd forgotten all about the barbecue. Usually it would be my idea of hell, but some of the locals have lived around here for decades and I'm greedy for more information about Colin. 'I'll be there.'

You've been panicking for nothing. It could be Colin's dead wife.

Except if it is Colin's dead wife, then I've been living practically next door to a murderer for a year. When Sam leaves I Google 'Colin Kembridge missing woman.'

There's nothing.

It's almost six when Manchee and I arrive at the barbecue. I was out moping in the nettle patch again, and lost track of time. It's being held on the grassy area in front of the village hall, and we take a shortcut through the graveyard. The majority of the headstones are furred with moss, and the names and dates etched on them are unreadable.

Morton-on-Spay is more of a hamlet than a village and there's not much to it: a church that's open just often enough to prevent it being sold off for housing, a few black and white medieval cottages that ooze oldy-worldy charm but are freezing in winter, a cluster of small farm workers' cottages and the barn conversions where Sam lives, and a few larger houses hidden snootily behind sculpted hedges. Demographically, it's whiter than snow, but it's diverse class-wise and can be cliquey. Manchee and I weave through the cliques dotted on the lawn looking for Sam and George. The air is ripe with the smells of summer: cut grass, charring chicken and wood smoke. I catch snippets of conversation en route. Everyone is talking about the body in the woods.

I join Sam and George, who are tucking into paper plates piled with black-skinned chicken pieces and coleslaw. I'm still nauseous, and I swallow a mouthful of saliva. I'm about to ask if the obese man with the poodle – the font of all Colin knowledge – is around, when he waddles up to join us. His chin is greasy and the dog is tucked under one meaty arm. George greets him heartily.

'You remember Claire, Johnny?' George says to him.

Johnny's eyes turn on me. They're bulbous and yellow-tinged. The dog in his arms looks first at me with its black button eyes, then stares down disdainfully at Manchee. 'You're in the old gamekeeper's cottage,' he says.

'I am.'

'So what do you... Right. What do you think of this business about the body, Johnny?' Sam asks.

'Ah well, that's quite the question, isn't it?'

'You knew Colin's wife, didn't you, Johnny?' George says. I know he's asking this for my benefit – after all, from what Sam said when she popped around earlier, George already knows these details.

Johnny doesn't answer immediately. I can tell he's enjoying holding court and wants to stretch out his performance. 'I met her briefly. She came from somewhere down south.'

'How... Right. How did they meet?' Sam asks.

'Now that I don't know. Alls I can tell you was that she moved in with Colin and his father. Didn't like her myself. Wasn't too friendly.' (Is it my imagination or does he glance at me when he says this?) 'Never saw or heard of any trouble with her. Suze knew her a bit better than me.'

'That's Johnny's wife,' Sam whispers loudly. 'She's... Right. Dead. Embolism.'

'And then she disappeared?' I ask, ignoring Sam.

'Colin told Suze his wife didn't like the life. Too quiet for her. Said she went back to her family.'

'But if the police have called him in, that means she didn't do that, right?' I suspect I'm sounding desperate, but I can't help it. *Please let the body they've found be Colin's dead wife.*

Johnny takes his time gazing at each of us in turn. His dog does the same, as if it's actually some kind of hyper-realistic hand puppet. 'No one came looking for her far as I know,' Johnny says. 'Colin's a good 'un. Never heard of him causing any trouble. Keeps himself to himself, but nothing wrong with that.' He waves in the direction of the graveyard. 'His father's buried here. Generations of the family are.'

The two posh women from the horse farm join us. They have identical greying bobs and rough, all-weather skin. 'You talking about the body?' the larger of the two says.

'We were talking about... Right. Colin,' Sam says.

'Poor old Colin,' the woman sighs. 'I don't believe for a second that he's guilty of anything. He's so helpful.' She turns to her partner. 'Remember when Missy was foaling and the vet got stuck on the driveway during the storm? Colin was there in a flash to help out.'

Her wife or girlfriend purses her lips, but I can't tell if this is in approval or disapproval.

The large woman touches George's arm. 'You used to be in the force, didn't you?'

George puffs out his chest, and Johnny and his dog seem to deflate. It's George's turn to bask in the attention. 'I did.'

'Well, we thought you should know, we heard and saw something suspicious a few weeks ago.'

George narrows his eyes. 'Did you? What?'

'It sounded like a car – a big one. It drove down our driveway. Late at night.' The woman does a mock shudder. 'What if it was the *killer* disposing of the body?'

Christ. It must have been Dean, trying to find my house. 'When was this exactly?' I ask, trying to sound nothing but mildly curious.

The large woman's partner shrugs. 'Can't be exact.'

'Did you tell this to the police?' George asks.

'Of course. They'll be checking the CCTV, I suppose.'

Shit, shit, shit, shit.

'There's none in this area, love.' George says. I could kiss him. 'Did you get a look at the driver?'

'No. We were in bed. Looked out of the window, saw it backing up the driveway. Well, its taillights anyway.'

Change the subject. 'How long can they keep Colin without charging him?' I ask George.

'Forty-eight hours unless they find more evidence.'

'What about his dog?' I ask.

'Going up there later to feed her,' Johnny says. 'Offered to have her at the house, but as she's a farm dog and Buttercup doesn't like other dogs in her territory' – the poodle perks up at the sound of her name – 'the police agreed to let her stay in Col's barn while they get on with it.'

It's the thought of the elderly dog being without her master that finally floods me with guilt about Colin, and I find myself offering to head up there to feed Clipper. If Colin isn't a wife-murderer and is being blamed for the body, *my* body, then feeding his dog is the least I can do.

I make my excuses and leave.

I've been steeling myself to encounter teams of white-suited SOCOs streaming all over Colin's place, but there's just a prepubescent policeman in uniform at the end of the driveway when I arrive. I tell him that I'm here for the dog, and he takes my name, says something into his radio, and tells me to go ahead. Manchee and I walk down the long, overgrown driveway. The house is hidden from the mountain bike parking area, and is surrounded by a couple of holding paddocks, several sagging outbuildings – one of which houses Clipper's kennel – and the rusty frame of an ancient Dutch barn. The place has a dark aura of neglect. There's a graveyard of rusting material on the lawn – old washing machines, the innards of an ancient tractor and a couple of cars covered with tatty tarpaulin. And Colin's garden, like mine, is showing signs of the virulent black algae that I haven't seen anywhere else in the area. I step over a rotten hosepipe that lies in a figure of eight in front of Clipper's shed.

Clipper's tail thumps sadly when she sees us approach. Manchee greets her respectfully, then goes to lie in the shade. Clipper's eyes are dull, muddy stones in her skull. I don't know where Colin keeps the food, so I've brought her some cooked liver in an old ice-cream tub. She eats it delicately at first, then inhales it. I refill her water bowl from the outside tap, noticing that that same insidious mould is creeping over the outside wall.

The house itself is larger than I expected, and must have once been a handsome stone building. I peer through the windows and into the kitchen, feeling like an intruder. The place is filthy, with stacks of newspaper and magazines piled everywhere like a hoarder's house. The room would once have been a glorious welcoming space, but someone – Colin presumably – has painted many of the surfaces with bright yellow oil-based paint. A drunken decision?

As Manchee and I say goodbye to Clipper, poor old lonely Clipper, a helicopter whips above our heads.

That night, Iain calls the landline. For the first time ever I've forgotten to Skype him. Iain, the man I've been with for four years now, has completely gone out of my head. The police have been in touch with him and he offers to come home immediately. I tell him there's no need.

'Aren't you scared?'

I think about it. 'No. Not at all.' It's true. Either there are two bodies in the woods: Colin's wife and my body. Or there's one body in the woods. My body.

When Iain hangs up I head outside. It's drizzling, but I barely feel it.

Twelve

They've found the rest of the skull, as well as 'other remains with signs of animal damage'. I've seen what foxes can do to a lamb and the odd deer that ends up dying in the woods. And what about the plastic that was wrapped around the corpse? There must be traces of that scattered around if the foxes burrowed into the grave. I wore gloves that night, but what if they test it for DNA? I've seen enough crime shows to know that a stray hair can seal your fate.

All they know is that it's 'a woman in her late fifties or early sixties.'

Mae. Please don't let it be Mae.

We were friends once.

Have I unwittingly buried the body of my friend? No. No. *No.*

I keep refreshing my browser, and finally a new story comes up on the *Daily Mail* site. There's speculation about 'a local man who has been taken in for questioning,' but they're nervous about saying too much after what happened to Christopher Jefferies. There's also a paragraph about how you can get a five bedroomed house in this area for the same price as a bedsit in

Camden.

I scroll down, and then I see it: Another picture, taken from the air, this time with better resolution.

It's the area housing my grave, a white peaked tent positioned off to one side.

So now I know for sure. It's definitely my body. I buried a woman in the woods.

Bastard, bastard Dean.

I grab the phone and I'm about to dial when common sense takes over. I can't call from here. I have to be cautious. Everyone who has ever watched a BBC crime drama knows that. There can be no connection between us.

What if it's Mae? Will you go to the police then, Claire?

I drive three villages away until I'm almost in Wales, and find a public phone box. It doesn't take coins and I have to go to the village shop to buy a phone card. *Will the shop woman remember you?*

Tough.

On my first attempt he doesn't pick up. I try again.

'This is Dean.'

'They've arrested someone,' I blurt. 'A man from one of the nearby farms.' Dead air. 'Did you hear me? He's innocent, Dean.'

'Then they'll let him go. Why did they arrest him?'

'They think the woman might be his wife. She disappeared, ran off, years ago.' Another silence. 'It's a woman, Dean. We buried a woman. You said it was a man.'

'I did not.' He sighs. 'You assumed it was a man and I went along with it.' That bloody shoe in the bloody boot had made me think it was man.

'Why did you lie?' *Stupid question.* 'Tell me the truth, Dean. Who is she?'

'Let's just see how this plays out.'

'*Plays out?* We're going to go to fucking prison, Dean. There's no way we'll get away with this.'

I picture Iain waiting for me on a hard bench outside an interrogation room, his face a picture of disgust and disappointment. I'll lose everything I've worked for. Iain. The house. Manchee. I'll lose everything.

'We'll be fine, Claire.'

'Yeah? Well the women next door to me heard a car coming down their driveway round about the same time you dropped in on me.' It hits me that he'd even lied about that – he'd asked me if there were other houses in the vicinity when he knew very well that there were. It was a small lie, but for some reason it riles me more than his other, more potentially catastrophic deceit.

Again he doesn't answer me.

'If they find out you were in the area, what should we say?'

'They won't.'

'What if they do?'

'Then we'll say that I'm an old friend and I decided to visit you on a whim. I was worried about my son and needed to talk.'

'You think they'll believe you drove three-and-a-half hours just for that?'

'Sure. Why not?'

'Dean. I have to know – is it Mae?'

A heavy pause, then: 'What? Are you serious? Of course not. She's on sabbatical. You honestly think I'd ask you to bury Mae?'

'There's nothing I'd put past you if I'm honest.'

'After all we've been through? After all I've done for you over the years?'

'Get off your high horse, Dean. We both know what you are.' I realise that I'm shouting, and I glance around in case a passer-by has heard me. The street is empty. Thank Christ for sleepy country villages. But I have to wrap this up – Manchee's in the car. I've left the windows open, but she can't be in there for much longer without overheating.

'Hold on.' I hear the Skype ring tone, and then, 'What's up, Dean?' It's Mae's voice – I instantly recognise her masculine tones. He says something about dialling her by accident, she says 'whatever, asshole' and then comes the whoop of the call ending.

'See?' he says. There's a note of triumph in his voice.

'Who is it then, Dean?'
'I don't know.'
'What do you mean you don't know?'
He ends the call.

Thirteen

Rat-tat-tat on the door.

I open up, expecting Sam, but it's Colin. I almost scream, then collect myself. I hastily check to see what I'm wearing. On a couple of occasions I've found myself wandering around the house with my shirt unbuttoned or inside out.

I don't know what to say. *So you're out then? Sorry for putting you through all of that, Colin. Totally my fault.* 'Colin!' I say, sounding too bright and over-friendly, as if I'm talking to a mental patient or someone recently bereaved. He doesn't look like he's been through the legal system. He doesn't look any different.

Weirdly, he's clutching a box of Quality Street.

He hands me the box of chocolates. 'This is for feeding the dog. John in the village said you did that. Good of you.'

'Oh… right. You're welcome.' Pause. 'Would you like some tea?'

'No. You're all right. By the by, your tree is dying.'

I'm instantly on the back foot. 'My tree? Which tree?'

'The big oak out the back. C'mon. I'll show you.'

He waits for me to pull on my boots, and I follow him up the mould-covered slabs. Even the fresh gravel Iain and I laid around the cottage is now looking shabby, weeds pushing up through it.

We reach the base of the tree. Colin points to a section midway up its trunk where a limb was once lopped off. A thick black substance is bleeding out of it. 'That's a sign that it's on its way out. Diseased, you see.'

'Shit.' I love this tree. It's one of the reasons we bought this place. *You killed it. It's been here for hundreds of years, yet you killed it with one act.* 'Is there nothing we can do to save it?'

'Pollarding it might work, but it'll be cheaper to take it down.' He turns away. He smears a boot over the mould on the concrete slabs. 'Bad that is.' He holds my gaze for once. 'I'll be going. Got things to sort out.'

I call Sam and George the second he leaves. Sam finds it difficult to talk on the phone so it's George who answers. It's George I want to talk to in any case. I tell him that I've just had a visit from Colin.

'Heard he'd been let out,' George says. 'Body can't be his wife's then. Maybe the dental records didn't match. Or maybe she came forward. Got him off the hook.' He clears his throat. 'Makes you wonder, doesn't it?'

'Wonder what?'

'Who she is, love. Just who was buried out there, and why.'

George says something else, but I miss it and have to ask him to repeat himself. 'I was asking if you're sure you're comfortable up there by yourself.'

'Thanks, but I'll be fine.' *After all, I know the killer, don't I?*

Iain is getting increasingly annoyed with me. I'm still forgetting to turn my Skype on and more than once I've called him hours later than I said I would. I go through the motions but it's like talking to someone from another life, another world. He keeps asking what's wrong with me, and says he thinks I'm depressed and should go and see someone. I refuse. This escalates into our first big fight. He threatens to break his contract and return home. I break the connection.

Maybe he's right. Maybe I am depressed. At least I haven't started self-medicating. Filling the shopping trolley with vodka or setting myself up for the day with a shot of whiskey. It's not just the stress and guilt of what I've done. I should have started work on the second guest cottage ages ago. Things are sliding. Everything's sliding. I haven't even bothered to see if my own bloody son needs anything. I'm ignoring my emails: there have been loads of enquiries about the finished cottage, and when I looked in the mirror last night I saw a bloated face, the shadow of a moustache on my top lip, a line of grey roots in my side parting.

Who did I bury in the woods?

Who?

She was on the news last night. They've done a facial reconstruction, piecing together the skull fragments and sculpting clay over them to get an idea of what she looked like when she was alive. She has high Slavic cheekbones, and a strong jaw. They've added dark glass eyes that stare mournfully into the far distance and a terrible synthetic wig that looks like it fell out of the 'eighties. She's not what you'd call attractive, and I hate myself for thinking this. It's a vile, unsisterly judgement.

A pic of the reconstructed head is up on the front page of most of the news sites, and I have it on my laptop screen now. I've been sitting here for so long staring into those dead eyes that my legs have gone to sleep, and the tingle as I move them echoes the stings on my palms.

This is the woman I buried, and I'm greedy for information about her.

According to the reports, the forensic experts believe she might have led a 'rather rough life'. Evidence from Isotope analysis implies that she was a heavy drinker, and the few teeth that Nelson hadn't crunched to powder when he found the jawbone show signs of poor dental care. Then there's the fact that no one has come forward to claim her. They're suggesting that she may have lived on the streets.

Why would Dean kill a woman who lived rough?

It makes no sense.

None of the news reports have mentioned a likely date of her death, so hopefully this can't be pinpointed.

That may be so, but you're not out of the woods just yet. Ahahahahahaha.

Manchee nudges my thigh. She needs to go out. Once again, I've been neglecting her.

'Hellloooooooo!'

Sam finds me scrabbling in the new nettle patch that's sprung up almost overnight next to the compost pit. A sticky mass of bindweed weaves amongst the plants.

Sam glances at my hands. My fingers are caked in soil and my palms are raw and puffy.

'You okay?'

'Yes.' I give her a sunny smile that I hope doesn't reflect the lunacy that's never far away.

'The…. Right. George says that the police have left. No…. Right. Resources.'

I should feel relief, but instead I'm indignant for the woman I buried. *If she weren't an anonymous fifty-something but a blonde teenager with a photogenic family, would they have given up searching for the rest of her so soon?*

She asks me if I feel like going for a walk. I don't, but I want the distraction, and Manchee is dying to get out of the garden. Yesterday, I caught her sniffing at the mould on the stairs. I think about asking Sam's advice on this, and my tomatoes, but decide against it.

'Shall we… Shall we go look at… Right. The place?'

I know what she means. 'Now?'

'Yes.'

My gut is screaming *no*. Don't go back there. But I need to see it.

We don't talk much, which is unusual for us, but I ask her about Colin and how he's doing. 'Did he say if he was treated well in jail?' I'm still guilty about that. *And rightly so.*

'No. Right... George asked him about it, but he said he didn't want to talk.'

We push through the bracken, and it springs back and bounces against my thighs, last night's rain soaking through my trousers. The spiked arm of a bramble pierces my skin. Sam goes first as we make our way to the depression in the ground. Will she remember that this is where I chased after Nelson the day after Dean and I buried the body in the woods?

She doesn't mention it.

There's the crack of a branch nearby. A figure approaches us. It's Colin. Of course it's Colin. The third player in the drama – fourth if you include the body. Clipper comes up to me, tail wagging at half-mast. She must remember me as the giver of liver.

Sam greets him just as effusively as always. 'Missed you at the... Right. At the barbecue,' she says to him, as if we didn't all know he was banged up at the time on account of his missing-possibly-dead wife.

Colin looks straight at me. 'This was where she was? The woman?'

'I believe so.' I sound forced, and – to my own ears at least – as guilty as fuck.

'Ah.' Colin says. He hawks, spits and then slopes away without saying goodbye.

Sam and I don't linger long, but on our way home, Sam's eyes never stop darting around the undergrowth.

'What are you looking for, Sam?'

But I know. I know what she's doing. She's looking for any remains that the police might have missed.

'I can't do this any more, Sam.'

'What?'

'Walk with you. I just can't.'

I call Manchee, then stalk away from her. Sam is too good. She's unsullied, pure, and I don't want to infect her. I don't deserve to be around anyone decent again.

Fourteen

I've been half-dozing on the couch when the phone shrieks. Manchee's asleep in her basket, but I'm on my feet in seconds. I check the time. Four a.m.

Oh God. *Iain. Something's happened to Iain. Or Jake — no. Not Jake. Not that.* A dark voice whispers nastily: *That would be a fitting punishment, wouldn't it?*

I snatch up the receiver, sick with trepidation.

'Have they been to see you?' It's Dean. The flood of relief that it's not horrible news about Jake or Iain is blasted away by fury at him. Then his actual words seep into my brain.

'Have who seen me?'

'The police.'

'Fuck. No. Why would they?'

'The car.'

'What car?'

'My car. The car I was driving that evening. The Merc.'

'What about it?'

'It was a lease. And when I returned it your address was on the Sat Nav. One of the car company's guys was resetting it, saw the address, remembered the name of the area from the news footage and called the police.'

'Fuck.' Plus, the livery stable women told the police about hearing a car coming down their driveway late one night. Late *that* night, although there's no way to prove that was when the body was dumped. I hope. 'And? Did they come and see you?'

'They did.'

'Did they *arrest* you?'

'No.'

'And?' It's like pulling teeth. I'm biting my lip so hard I can taste blood.

'They'll be coming to talk to you. I told them that you and I were having an affair.'

'You told them *what?*'

'Just go along with it. Why else would I visit at that time of night? There's no proof. There's no connection to the incident.'

'I have to see you, Dean.'

'No. Just go along with it, it'll all work out. Look, I won't call you again. I'm only doing it now because I'm sure they won't be watching me at this time of night.'

'Why did you kill her, Dean?'

'I didn't kill her, Claire. For fuck sakes, I've told you this.'

A pause, then the phone goes dead. Some part of my brain registers that this is the first time I've ever heard Dean swear.

I scratch at the nettle stings on my palms as I pace back and forth. *Fuck.*

Call Iain. Tell Iain the truth. Tell him the truth. Come clean.

No. I can't.

They'll search the cottage. My jeep. They'll take my laptop. Check my search history – you can't erase everything unless you destroy the hard drive. And I was Googling missing people days before the body was unearthed. Circumstantial, but still. And we practically put Colin in the frame for it. They could come at anytime.

Oh fuck, I whisper over and over again. But there's also an element of relief. One way or another, it'll all be over soon.

No one comes to interrogate me, but I get another phone call, this one from a woman who introduces herself as Detective Constable Grant. She sounds rushed and distracted, as if she's checking the time as we speak and gets straight into it. She asks me if I know Dean Warren and if I'll confirm that he came to see me two months ago.

I tell her that yes, I vaguely remember him visiting me a while ago, but I can't remember the exact date. I do, however, let slip that I'd rather my husband not know about Dean's visit. I'm amazed at my performance. I sound just guilty enough to be believable. She can't see that I've had to sit down while I talk as my legs won't hold me up; my body once again taking the brunt of my deceit. After a pause, she says that discretion shouldn't be a problem.

After the police officer hangs up, I immediately Skype Iain as a mental palate cleanser. Once more, I can feel the distance between us. Not just geographically, but emotionally. It's almost like talking to a stranger, but I'm becoming a good actress. This time, he doesn't ask me what's wrong. We're both tip-toeing around each other; aware that whatever we have is far more fragile than we thought. I tell him about the tree, and that Colin is out of prison. He asks the question I haven't considered until now: 'Did they find his wife?'

'No. I don't think so.' George had wondered if she might have come forward to clear Colin, but I'd heard nothing to indicate she had. 'They can't have found any proof that she's dead in any case. And she's not the body in the woods.'

The connection breaks up.

I wander outside to check on the tomatoes. The greenhouse lets out a guff of warm air that smells almost like rotting meat when I open the door. The rest of the fruit is now blackened, the skin on many of the tomatoes split and seeping, and the strange fungus has begun to eat right through the stalks. I should rip them up and chuck them on the compost pile.

The nettles have begun to spring up in the far corner of the yard.

Now the body in the woods has gone, why is the garden still poisoned?

All in your mind.

It's not.

It is.

There are a slew of emails waiting for me when I return to the house – more enquiries about the cottage. Perhaps they're from people eager to sniff around the gravesite and embark on a spot of dark tourism. Sickos. I delete them, unread.

The couple that rented the cottage have written a lovely, gushing review about their stay. I didn't expect that of them. It makes me want to cry.

I can't do it anymore. I can't live like this. I can't not *know*. I grab my keys and call Manchee and she flings herself into the back of the car.

I drive to the next village and take Manchee for a spin around one of the neighbouring fields. A family is picnicking next to the river, and they look up at me and smile. I have a sudden urge to confess to them, to scream: *I buried that woman in the woods!* Instead I return their smile as if I'm a normal person and walk further along the bank so that Manchee can have a dip in the water.

On my way home I stop at a phone box and call Dean. I dial and dial and dial but he doesn't pick up. I leave a message: 'Tell me the truth. Tell me who she is or I will go to the police. I'm serious.'

One a.m.

I've disabled the sensor lights in the endless quest to get a good night's sleep, so it's the crunch of boots on gravel that alerts me to the fact that there's someone out there. Manchee lets out a half-hearted woof.

I'm so tired I can only muster up the faintest spark of fear. I don't care what happens to me now. *Bring it on.* Whoever's outside – and who else can it be but Dean? – must be able to see the bluish flicker of the TV screen through the window and will know I'm at home.

In the countryside, no one can hear you scream.

I wait for the door to be kicked in, the window to be smashed. Nothing. Instead, a piece of paper is pushed under the front door, followed by the crunch, crunch, crunch of retreating footsteps. Now I can make out the faint burr of an engine. He must have coasted down the driveway when he arrived here, his engine off, but you can't coast back up.

I make myself get up from my nest on the couch to collect it. It's a letter. A typed letter that I'm pretty sure will have been penned on an anonymous computer and be devoid of fingerprints. I half-expect to see 'burn after reading' scrawled across the top in red ink.

It was done to pay back a debt. An associate, someone I used to do business with, asked me to help him out. He says he didn't mean to kill her. An accident. He was racing back from a meeting, drunk, and hit her when she crossed in front of his car.

He knew that if there was a body, there would be an investigation. He took the body.

He asked me to do him a favour. I agreed.

I asked you to do me a favour. You agreed.

We both paid our debts.

There is no case against me. I have no connection to this woman. She's no one. It won't go any further.

We're in the clear.

I won't contact you again.

This is the truth.

I scrunch the letter up and throw it on the fire. I call up *Step Brothers* on Netflix – the most distracting movie I can think of – and curl up on the couch next to Manchee.

She's no one.

Everyone's someone.

Block it out.

But is it the truth?

Does it matter?

No.

The definition of being a good friend is helping someone bury a body in the woods, no questions asked.

Fifteen

It's been three months since I buried the body in the woods. People have lost interest in the story, and there's nothing new online about the unfortunate woman. No one has come forward to claim her as a friend or a family member. It's obvious that she was one of the 'missing missing', someone who'd fallen through society's cracks long before she ended up on my doorstep, via Dean.

She's no one.

Stop it.

Iain comes home tomorrow. I'm not sure how I feel about this. I keep rehearsing what I'll say to him. The truth is out of the question, but I can't decide if I should suggest that we sell up, find another old property in need of love and fix that up. Leave this place behind. This place is poisoned because of what I did, but maybe I deserve to stay here. It'll be a punishment. The only one I'm likely to get.

Because no one has come for me. No police officers; no reporters. No one.

Dean was right. I have got away with it. He has got away with it, too. Again.

I rest my elbows on the kitchen counter and watch a slug slicking a slimy trail across the breadboard. The mould is spreading to the house's interior, and I'm forced to spend an hour every couple of days scrubbing it away. If I stay, I'll have to learn to live with this sort of thing.

Manchee pads up to me and nudges my thigh with her nose. Time for a walk. She's as downbeat as I am these days, as if we feed off each other emotionally. Her coat is duller than it once was. For the last two weeks, she's only picked at her food. She deserves better than me, but as I'm all she's got, I grab her lead and head out.

Summer has slid into autumn, and the leaves are turning. The cancerous oak is shedding its leaves alarmingly fast: the last ones it will ever have. The brown and golden curls have clogged the drainpipe next to the guest cottage. I went in there earlier today. It smelled foetid. The inside of the toilet bowl was black, crusted with a coating of that mysterious filth. I shut the lid and backed out of there.

Sam has stopped popping over to collect me on her walks. I shouldn't have snapped at her like that, but perhaps it's for the best.

'We'll be walking alone again today, Manchee.'

She ignores me, and snuffles off on the trail of a rabbit or a fox. She'll catch up with me. She knows where I'm going. Where I always go these days.

I pick my way to the gravesite. The area around it is clear of foliage and broken branches, but there's still a scrap of yellow police tape hanging like a sad flag from one of the trees. I sink to my haunches next to the hole and dig my hands into the earth, letting the soil worm its way beneath my nails.

Seconds, minutes, maybe hours later – I've drifted off into my own semi-mad reverie – I'm aware of a presence next to me. I look up. It's Colin. I've been so hypnotised by the hole that I haven't heard him approaching. He looms over me. I haven't seen him for weeks.

I say the words before I'm even aware of what I'm doing: 'I'm sorry, Colin.'

'Ah, you mean the dog?'

'Huh?'

'Had to put Clipper down.'

'I'm sorry.'

'It was her time. She was a good 'un.'

Silence. Then, I hear a yip of glee in the distance. Manchee must be closing in on her prey. Colin makes no move to leave.

'I'm sorry for all the trouble you went through, Colin. The arrest and that.'

He snorts. 'Oh, that.'

His face is in shadow now. It's getting darker earlier these days. Have I got anything left to lose? *Ask it.* 'Did you kill her, Colin? Your wife?'

'Yes.'

I'm calm. And curiously, completely relaxed. 'Is she buried here?' I'm whispering like an ingénue. 'In the woods?'

Colin shakes his head, then laughs. 'Nah. Fed her to the pigs.' He gives me a small, knowing salute. And then he walks away.

I don't go home. I lie in the depression that Dean and I dug all those weeks ago.

Quiet. Still. And then, a thin screeching sound. It's high and despairing and almost human and cuts through the silence. Manchee has finally caught a rabbit.

Something skitters over my face. I shut my eyes.

For the first time in months I feel at peace. A body in the woods.

About the Author

Sarah Lotz is a pulp fiction novelist and screenwriter with a fondness for the macabre and fake names. Her collaborative and solo novels have been translated into over twenty-five languages. She currently lives in a forest with her family and other animals.

NewCon Press Novellas, Set 2

Simon Clark / Alison Littlewood / Sarah Lotz / Jay Caselberg

Cover art by Vincent Sammy

Case of the Bedevilled Poet ~ His life under threat, poet Jack Crofton flees through the streets of war-torn London. He seeks sanctuary in a pub and falls into company with two elderly gentlemen who claim to be the real Holmes and Watson. Unconvinced but desperate, Jack shares his story, and Holmes agrees to take his case…

Cottingley ~ A century after the world was rocked by news that two young girls had photographed fairies in the sleepy village of Cottingley, we finally learn the true nature of these fey creatures. Correspondence has come to light; a harrowing account written by village resident Lawrence Fairclough that lays bare the fairies' sinister malevolence.

Body in the Woods ~ When an old friend turns up on Claire's doorstep one foul night and begs for her help, she knows she should refuse, but she owes him and, despite her better judgement, finds herself helping to bury something in the woods. Will it stay buried, and can Claire live with the knowledge of what she did that night?

The Wind ~ Having moved to Abbotsford six months ago, Gerry reckons he's getting used to country life and the rural veterinary practice he's taken on. Nothing prepared him, though, for the strange wind that springs up to stir the leaves in unnatural fashion, nor for the strikingly beautiful woman the villagers are so reluctant to talk about…

NewCon Press Novellas, Set 1

Alastair Reynolds – The Iron Tactician

A brand new stand-alone adventure featuring the author's long-running character Merlin. The derelict hulk of an old swallowship found drifting in space draws Merlin into a situation that proves far more complex than he ever anticipated.
Released December 2016

Simon Morden – At the Speed of Light

A tense drama set in the depths of space; the intelligence guiding a human-built ship discovers he may not be alone, forcing him to contend with decisions he was never designed to face.
Released January 2017

Anne Charnock – The Enclave

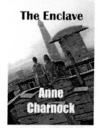

A new tale set in the same milieu as the author's debut novel *A Calculated Life*". The Enclave: bastion of the free in a corporate, simulant-enhanced world…shortlisted for the 2013 Philip K. Dick Award.
Released February 2017

Neil Williamson – The Memoirist

In a future shaped by omnipresent surveillance, why are so many powerful people determined to wipe the last gig by a faded rock star from the annals of history? What are they afraid of?
Released March 2017

All cover art by Chris Moore

www.newconpress.co.uk

NEWCON PRESS

Publishing quality Science Fiction, Fantasy, Dark Fantasy and Horror for ten years and counting.

Winner of the 2010 'Best Publisher' Award from the European Science Fiction Society.

Anthologies, novels, short story collections, novellas, paperbacks, hardbacks, signed limited editions, e-books… Why not take a look at some of our other titles?

Featured authors include:
Neil Gaiman, Brian Aldiss, Kelley Armstrong, Peter F. Hamilton, Alastair Reynolds, Stephen Baxter, Christopher Priest, Tanith Lee, Joe Abercrombie, Dan Abnett, Nina Allan, Sarah Ash, Neal Asher, Tony Ballantyne, James Barclay, Chris Beckett, Lauren Beukes, Aliette de Bodard, Chaz Brenchley, Keith Brooke, Eric Brown, Pat Cadigan, Jay Caselberg, Ramsey Campbell, Simon Clark, Michael Cobley, Genevieve Cogman, Storm Constantine, Hal Duncan, Jaine Fenn, Paul di Filippo, Jonathan Green, Jon Courtenay Grimwood, Frances Hardinge, Gwyneth Jones, M. John Harrison, Amanda Hemingway, Paul Kane, Leigh Kennedy, Nancy Kress, Kim Lakin-Smith, David Langford, Alison Littlewood, James Lovegrove, Una McCormack, Ian McDonald, Sophia McDougall, Gary McMahon, Ken MacLeod, Ian R MacLeod, Gail Z. Martin, Juliet E. McKenna, John Meaney, Simon Morden, Mark Morris, Anne Nicholls, Stan Nicholls, Marie O'regan, Philip Palmer, Stephen Palmer, Sarah Pinborough, Gareth L. Powell, Robert Reed, Rod Rees, Andy Remic, Mike Resnick, Mercurio D. Rivera, Adam Roberts, Justina Robson, Lynda E. Rucker, Stephanie Saulter, Gaie Sebold, Robert Shearman, Sarah Singleton, Martin Sketchley, Michael Marshall Smith, Kari Sperring, Brian Stapleford, Charles Stross, Tricia Sullivan, E.J. Swift, David Tallerman, Adrian Tchaikovsky, Steve Rasnic Tem, Lavie Tidhar, Lisa Tuttle, Simon Kurt Unsworth, Ian Watson, Freda Warrington, Liz Williams, Neil Williamson, and many more.

Join our mailing list to get advance notice of new titles and special offers:
www.newconpress.co.uk

IMMANION PRESS

Purveyors of Speculative Fiction
www.immanion-press.com

The Lightbearer by Alan Richardson

Michael Horsett parachutes into Occupied France before the D-Day Invasion. He is dropped in the wrong place, miles from the action, badly injured, and totally alone. He falls prey to two Thelemist women who have awaited the Hawk God's coming, attracts a group of First World War veterans who rally to what they imagine is his cause, is hunted by a troop of German Field Police who are desperate to find him, and has a climactic encounter with a mutilated priest who believes that Lucifer Incarnate has arrived…

The Lightbearer is a unique gnostic thriller, dealing with the themes of Light and Darkness, Good and Evil, Matter and Spirit.

"*The Lightbearer is another shining example of Alan Richardson's talent as a story-teller. An unusual and gripping war story with more facets than a star sapphire.*" – *Mélusine Draco, author of "Aubry's Dog" and "Black Horse, White Horse".* ISBN: 978-1-907737-63-3 £11.99 $18.99

Dark in the Day, Ed. by Storm Constantine & Paul Houghton

Weirdness lurks beyond the margins of the mundane, emerging to dismantle our assumptions of reality. Dark in the Day is an anthology of weird fiction, penned by established writers and also those new to the genre – the latter being authors who are, or were, students of Creative Writing at Staffordshire University, where editor Storm Constantine occasionally delivers guest lectures. Her co-editor, Paul Houghton, is the senior lecturer in Creative Writing at the university.

Contributors include: Martina Bellovičová, J. E. Bryant, Glynis Charlton, Storm Constantine, Louise Coquio, Elizabeth Counihan, Krishan Coupland, Elizabeth Davidson, Siân Davies, Paul Finch, Rosie Garland, Rhys Hughes, Kerry Fender, Andrew Hook, Paul Houghton, Tanith Lee, Tim Pratt, Nicholas Royle, Michael Marshall Smith, Paula Wakefield, Ian Whates and Liz Williams.

ISBN: 978-1-907737-74-9 £11.99, $18.99

Lightning Source UK Ltd.
Milton Keynes UK
UKOW03f2333230517
301878UK00001B/136/P